MW01101961

No More Dragons

Skaha Lake Middle School Library

by Rie Charles

Best wishes —
Rie Charles

Napoleon

Text © 2010 Rie Charles

All rights reserved. No part of this publication may be reproduced, stored in a retrieval system or transmitted, in any form or by any means, digital, mechanical, photocopying, recording or otherwise, without the prior consent of the publisher.

Cover design by Emma Dolan

Le Conseil des Arts | The Canada Council
du Canada | for the Arts

We acknowledge the support of the Canada Council for the Arts for our publishing program. We acknowledge the financial support of the Government of Canada through the Canada Book Fund for our publishing activities.

Napoleon Publishing
an imprint of Napoleon & Company
Toronto, Ontario, Canada
www.napoleonandcompany.com

14 13 12 11 10   5 4 3 2 1

Library and Archives Canada Cataloguing in Publication

Charles, Rie, date-
        No more dragons / Rie Charles.

ISBN 978-1-926607-12-2

        I. Title.

PS8635.I3775N6 2010   jC813'.6   C2010-905008-8

for
I, M, B & G
with love

October 11

Dear Graham,

I'm writing because it's starting to get to me. Plus I need to tell someone. It's my dad. I'm sure you'll keep a secret. I know I'm pretty dumb and a bad hockey player, but he doesn't need to tell me all the time. Right?

Like on Friday night, driving home from hockey practice, he said, "Why don't you dig in the corners? You lazy or something? Huh? Huh?" He jerked his head towards me. I could already feel the whack across my chest. "You a coward? Afraid of getting hurt? How could I have a dumb-dumb like you for a son?"

You know, sometimes I sort of want the hit to come. That sounds crazy. But it's like he has to bash something. At least then I know he'll be calmer. I scrunch down and wait. This time, just as he got out of the car, it came.

"Don't you grin at me, you." Bang. I guess he thought I was grinning at *him*. But I'd just been thinking how lucky I was to have made it home without another whack. Or so I thought. I stayed slumped down, holding myself in.

I hate hockey most of the time. But Dad won't let me quit. He forced me into it in Grade Two, and it's obvious I'm never going to be good. But he says all boys play hockey, and he won't have his son not playing.

Mom came out as Dad stomped into the house.

1

"How'd hockey go, love?" She smiled with just the corners of her mouth. I grunted in reply. I think she knew. I wish she would do something about him. Leave, preferably. I wish I could do something, but what's a thirteen-year-old like me supposed to do?

Mom helped me in with my hockey bag. Dad never does. Between the car and the house, I had wobbly legs and my body seemed to have to push through thick glue-air. But opening the door brought a simmering spaghetti sauce welcome. My mom's a good cook. Don't you think spaghetti sauce tickles your nose? The smell, that is? All those onions and celery, green pepper and tomatoes, garlic and stuff bubbling together.

But Dad, of course, yelled as we came in, "Where's dinner? How come it's not ready?"

Mom hung up her coat in the closet. And Dad's. He'd thrown his over the banister. "Tobey's not well. I got behind in my work. We'll be eating in ten minutes. I just need to cook the pasta, that's all."

"The least you could do is have supper on the table when a man gets home." Dad plunked himself in front of the TV. I never realized before how much Mom seems to know exactly when he's going to walk in the door. Like she has ESP.

"What do you mean Tobey's not well, Mom?" I laid the plates on the table, the glasses too. They clunked as I grabbed them, two in each hand.

"His belly hurts again, dear. But not to worry. I just used it as an excuse for being late." She jerked her head in the direction of the living room, indicating you know who.

"But Dad always says Tobey's had a miracle cure."

Mom rolled her eyes, the same huge brown eyes as Tobey's. Mine too, I guess. She gave me a hug. She doesn't have to bend down to hug me any more. Soon it'll be me bending down to her.

"You know your dad. He has to be in control of everything. But he can't be with cancer, so he just denies it's happening. Maybe he thinks it'll come true if he says that kind of thing." I don't understand half of what Mom says.

Just then Tobey bumped down the stairs and threw himself in my arms. "Sup-puh-ghetti!!" He laughed and I laughed and we bounced around Mom together. Boy, for a sick little kid, he's sure great. Always a smile. So how come he got sick, and I didn't? How come I'm the no-good loser, and he's the one who makes everyone laugh, grinning from elbow to elbow?

The next thing we knew, there was Bronson, snuffling his nose into our dance, yellowy brown tail wagging. He's a golden retriever and, for a dog, not too smelly. Then Margie piled down the stairs and jumped on a chair, singing "Baby Beluga in the deep blue sea, Swim so wild and you swim so free," at full yell.

Chaos. No wonder Dad bellowed from the living room for us to be quiet.

That was Friday. Now it's Sunday evening and Thanksgiving. We had turkey and pumpkin pie at Grandma Crispin's. It was okay. I guess I have lots to be thankful for, but sometimes I wonder. Hope you had a good Thanksgiving. Sorry. I'm not in a good mood.

That's all for now.

Alex

October 14

Dear Graham,

It's starting to feel almost like winter. Most of the leaves have blown off the trees, and everything looks cold and grey. Things feel dark and dead.

You'll never guess what happened in class today. Or maybe you would, knowing me. I came into the room as usual, sort of slouched down, trying not to be noticed. Everyone was really rowdy, so I knew Mrs. Mayo was away. She's always here before us kids get off the bus, and I wonder if that's because she knows this kind of thing might happen. There was Jeff. Jeffrey Pinsent with his spiky hair, pimply face and smudge of a mustache. And definitely no teacher.

"Hey, Crispin. Get your fat ass in here and shut up." The Grade Eight room was meant to be an Art Room, so it has an oversized cupboard at the back where the supplies of paper and paint and stuff are kept for the entire school. Before I knew it, he just up and shoved me into the open cupboard and threw the bolt. I wanted to say I'm not fat, because I'm not. In fact, Mom says I'm skinny. But Jeff usually acts even meaner, like I get really plowed, if I fight back. So I did nothing. I just crouched there until I heard the supply teacher calling out the roll call.

At "Crispin, Alex", I banged on the door and shouted,

"Present." I could hear giggles. The lock turned and a glare of light came in. I blinked.

"Are you Alex Crispin? What are you doing in here? Why aren't you in your seat?"

Three questions I couldn't answer with one word, so I said nothing and sat down. It was obvious who I was and that I hadn't locked myself in, so why bother answering anyway? She just said, "I'll see you at recess," and went on calling out names.

Of course at recess I had to talk. I had to tell her who put me in the cupboard. I couldn't just say nothing. There will definitely be more trouble from Jeff.

I bet guys don't do that to you, do they? You would just beat them up and mash their noses to a pulp if they tried anything stupid. That's what I want to do. But I guess Dad's right. I'm a coward. Plus I'd probably lose. A coward and a loser.

Alex

October 22

Dear Gray,

Is it all right if I call you that for short? I much prefer Alex to Alexander, so I figured you might be the same. Anyways, I thought I'd write once a week. Maybe that's too much for you. I suppose it depends on what happens, though. I also told myself I wouldn't write so much bad stuff. Yes, I'm writing to you to get junk off my chest so I feel better. But I don't think you'd want to listen if it's all bad. So from now on I will try to write good stuff mostly.

I wish you would write back, though. I know you can't, but I still wish you would. I pretend I can see you opening my letter in your room. You've got hockey posters on the wall. The bed has a great big puffy blue and green cover. You're curled up in the middle, reading, like I'm your best friend in the world and you want to know every detail of my life.

You definitely are my best friend. That's because I don't have a best friend here. Not even a friend, really. That's an awful thing to say. But it's true. It's hard living in the country. If there isn't someone your age who lives close by, you have to depend on your parents to drive you. In the summer you can cycle, if the other person doesn't live too far away.

But Jeff, Alan (that's Jeff's pudgy sidekick) and Jordan

are the only guys in my class on my bus, the only guys my age who live even remotely near me. And they wouldn't want me to be a friend even if I wanted it. As if.

So why don't you move here? Better still. I could move to the city. I like that idea.

Later. A

October 28

Dear Graham,

For the past week, Mom, Margie and I have been making a Halloween costume for Tobey. He said he wants to be a butterfly. Mom bought a piece of white Bristol board and drew two huge wings joined together in the middle then drew a bunch of lines to make it look like a monarch butterfly in one of Dad's books. You know, monarchs are those orange and black butterflies that fly all the way to a valley in Mexico each fall.

Now every night Margie and I are on the floor colouring. I don't know how many magic markers we've used but I'm sure it must be half of all the orange and black in Whistler's Corners. I gave Margie the orange parts to do. That way if she goes outside the line, I can colour over in black. But so far so good. She's a good colourer.

Last night Tobey danced around us, getting in our way. "Are you finished yet? Are you finished yet?" He bounced up and down. "What is it? What is it?"

"A butterfly. You said you wanted to be a butterfly." He got down on the floor, head cocked to one side, and slid his fingers around the edges of the bristol board, feeling the curves.

"What's a butterfly?" he said.

I wanted to ask why he wanted to be a butterfly if he didn't know what it was. Instead I said, "You know those bugs about half the size of your hands with big flappy wings? Those are butterflies."

Tobey ran his hand over his head as he listened. His hair used to be what Mom called a deep, burnt red. After the chemo it all fell out. Now there's only a browny grey fuzz. I bent over and gave him a butterfly kiss on his forehead the way Mom does. He giggled.

"And do you know what?" I added. "Butterflies start out as those creepy crawlies that climb over your toes. The ones you don't want us to squish. They roll themselves up in a whole bunch of silky stuff and lie for a bit until, *voilà*, they push themselves out as beautiful butterflies."

Tobey just sat there staring off into space for ages and ages when I told him that. He can't see much. The tumor from his cancer has pressed on the nerve to his eyes and made him mostly blind. Now he sees just a lot of black and white, the doctors say, and just out of the rods. Or is it the cones? Anyway, the part of the eye that sees black and white and shapes, I think.

For Halloween Margie wants to be a bunch of grapes. She's got it all figured out. We're going to blow up lots of green balloons and attach them somehow from her shoulders. I'll have to go with them, so I'd better start thinking about my own costume. Do you go out for Halloween? I know I wouldn't be allowed to if I didn't have a younger brother and sister. I guess there are definite benefits to having them around.

There you are. I wrote a whole letter without com-
plaining.

Talk to you later.

a

October 29

Hi G,

I didn't plan on writing so soon, but I thought I'd tell you some exciting news. Mrs. Mayo reminded us today that she always has her class put on a play at the end of the year. I'd just love to be in it. I've never been in a school production before, let alone a real play. Well, I guess our class always does something for the holiday pageant like sing "Jingle Bells" or something, but that's different.

There's something so exciting and real about plays. It definitely sounds funny to use the word "real" about something that's just pretend. But it's like the actors are making a story right there on the spot. I think I'd like to be an actor and a writer when I grow up. Does that sound weird? I've never even seen a real play before, but I just know it would thrilling to be on a big stage or, if I wrote something, to hear my own words said by professionals.

Dad says I'm not brainy enough to do anything decent. He says Margie's got a lot more brains, and she's going to catch up to me in school. Of course that's not true. Even though she skipped and is in Grade Three, she's only seven and a whole lot younger than me. But still, I wish he wouldn't say that.

Plus, I'm pretty sure he wouldn't approve of acting.

But when I think about it, he probably wouldn't approve of anything I did.

Anyways, the play will be at the end of April, and we have to audition for a part. The audition is in January, I think. If we aren't in the play, we do things like lighting and making props. Mrs. Mayo, of course, is the director. I'm really looking forward to it. The only thing I don't like is that the whole class has to be involved, and that means Jeff and Alan.

Do you know what you do for an audition? How you go about it? Have you ever done one? I probably won't have the nerve to act something out in front of Mrs. Mayo.

Gotta run. It's supper time.

Alexander the Actor (yeah, right!)

Nov. 2, Tuesday

Dear G,

We had a great Halloween. Did you? I took Tobey and Margie to all the farms and houses down our road. Dad was home (yuck, yuck and more yuck), but it meant Mom could drive us.

If I do say so myself, we did a fantastic job on Tobey's costume. To make that butterfly was a crazy amount of work, colouring all those shapes. On both sides too. But Tobey looked good in his green pants, jacket and black toque. We tied shoelaces through holes in the Bristol board—one lace around his middle and one over his shoulders, and his wings flapped away.

Margie's balloons hung on different lengths of string from a circle of cardboard that went over her head. She had to make do with purple grapes because Mom couldn't find any green balloons in town. Margie wasn't too happy, because she says she hates purple grapes. "That's lucky. You won't want to eat yourself then," I said. Pretty dumb joke. She gave me her best you-must-be-from-Mars look.

For me, I cut holes for my head and arms in a large, upside-down, white cardboard box and decorated it with knobs and dials. I wore all black—pants, gloves, Dad's old sweater—to match my slicked back hair and to contrast with the box. Then I pinned an old electrical cord to my chest so it hung down at the side. That was me, a basic radio.

The only problem was trying to drive with a radio, a butterfly and a bunch of grapes crammed into a small hatchback. The grapes flew around and bounced off the ceiling, hitting Mom's head from behind. And if the balloons weren't also hiding the back window, the butterfly wings were flapping in Mom's face. Besides, have you ever tried to put a seat belt on a butterfly? Every time we got in, it happened all over again. I nearly peed myself laughing.

Plus, even though Tobey's only five, or maybe BECAUSE he's five, he makes up jokes that really aren't funny. He laughs and laughs. Then we laugh, mainly at him. Then he repeats the joke and the giggling starts all over again.

We had so much candy to eat, I could feel my teeth rotting.

I'll write soon,

a

Nov. 5, Friday

Dear Graham,

This is definitely soon. I didn't say I would ONLY write good stuff, did I?

Today I need to write about bad stuff. That's a warning. I don't want to tell Mom. I'm afraid she'll be ashamed of me, think I'm a wuss. No, that's not fair. Dad would. He would say, just go beat them up yourself. If I tell Mom, she would probably tell the principal. That would be worse still.

When I told the supply teacher last month about Jeff locking me in the cupboard, she just said "Boys will be boys," and shrugged. I felt she looked at me as if I was a loser. Sort of like Dad. if I don't punch the other guy out in hockey, I'm not a real man.

Me, I like reading. I like making things and fixing things, sort of putzing around outdoors. I wander back in the field and even climb trees. I'm not so much into computer games. I like playing with Tobey. He's fun, even though he's so little. Last summer him and me (mostly me of course) made a tree fort. We found old boards out at the back of Lopatecki's barn and used the old Melba apple tree in our backyard because it has lots of spreading branches. We nailed some of the two-by-fours into the arms of the tree and found thin planks for a platform. Then we made high sides around it so that Tobey wouldn't fall off. The ladder was a bit crooked, but it worked.

He loves it. He climbs up there and stares off in the distance as if he's the captain of some old ship, looking for icebergs off the Newfoundland coast, like he's my great-great grandfather who Mom always talks about. I wonder how much Tobey sees. I worry he'll fall through one of the boards. Of course he's not allowed to climb up when I'm not there. Neither is Margie, but she does anyway. But mostly I worry that something's going to happen to him. I don't know what. I just feel it. And I don't know what I'd do.

I go to the tree fort by myself too. Next summer I'll even write letters to you up there. Anyway, that's me. What I'm trying to say is I'm pretty happy on my own. Yes, it'd be nice to have a real friend to talk to and do things with. But I'm still happy on my own.

I guess I'm avoiding telling you about what happened today. I'll get to the point right now.

At lunch Jeff and Alan finally got me. I usually turn around and go the other way if I see them coming. Or stay in the library at lunch. But today it was sunny and warm, for November, that is, and I wanted to be outside. I was just out the door and the next thing I knew, I was face down, eating dirt.

"You'll get worse than this if you go to the teachers again, wimp!" That was Jeff.

Of course I didn't. And won't. But the good news, I realized afterwards, is that Jeff must have got into trouble, or he wouldn't have known that I said who locked me in. Maybe teachers do listen.

But what made my day even worse was that it's Friday. For you, Friday is probably the best day of the week. No more school for two whole days. For me, Tuesday to Thursday is great because Dad's off in the city working. But Friday night means he comes home. The first thing he said when he walked in the door was, "How come you haven't piled up all that wood?" He looked right at me.

I said, "Because I've been busy, Dad."

He clouted me across the head. "I don't want any backtalk. What kind of busy is playing dress-up with Tobey and Margie?" First of all, I wasn't playing dress-up. They were. Second of all, Mom had called me in from piling up the wood to keep an eye on the kids. And third, keeping them out of her hair meant she could get supper ready on time. *For him.* I said nothing. It's sort of the same as with Jeff. If you say anything, it gets worse.

"Being a mommy's boy again, are you?" He looked at Mom. "Turning him into a girl are you, Julie?" He has a way of curling up his lip and smirking that I just hate. Plus he pronounces her name with a hard 'J' sound rather than the nice soft French 'je' she prefers. I stood in front of her. I thought he might take a swing at us. But he didn't—this time.

"Get out of my sight, you useless idiot. Do I have to do everything around here? Now I'm going to have to pile the wood tomorrow. All I do is work hard for you people all week, and you do nothing. Absolutely nothing. Why do I bother?"

"I'll do it, Dad," I said. I knew I should have done it yesterday and not left it to the last minute. I should have known.

Mom got into her make-Dad-happy mode. "You're right, dear. You do work awfully hard. We *are* grateful. It's just that I know how much you like to have your dinner ready on the table when you walk in. So I asked Alex to keep the little ones occupied for me. It's my fault, not his."

By the time she finished talking, she'd guided him over to his chair, and handed him the newspaper while motioning us to get ourselves *tout de suite* out of the room. Margie and Tobey were already sneaking upstairs. I tiptoed around the table to finish setting it. Dad didn't even approve of that. He glared at me with a you're-definitely-turning-into-a-girl look. But I figure anything's better than turning into him.

Sorry about this, G. I just had to tell you. You know, that's my biggest fear—turning into my dad.

Alex

November 10, Wednesday

Hi Graham,

It's the middle of the week, so life is better. And I just had to write to tell you what my sister did with Bronson.

He's really Margie's dog. She's supposed to feed him and let him out if he wants to pee or poop. This also means letting him back in. Saturday I was doing a bit of homework in the house and she was messing around outside, probably climbing in the tree fort or doing something else she's not supposed to do, when Bronson started barking, saying "enough of this outside weather". He wanted in. Margie went to the front porch and dragged his paw up to the door bell. She pushed his paw hard against it. I ran to the door, wondering who was there, and in bounded Bronson.

Later that afternoon, Bronson wanted out again so Margie let him out, and pushed his paw against the doorbell when he wanted back in. Then she whipped around the house and in through the back door and opened the front one for him. I think they must have done that a few more times.

Margie was soon going around saying, "See? I told you Bronson was smart." Then she'd giggle.

"Yeah, yeah," says me.

Well, Sunday morning she let him out the same as always, and guess what? He pushed the doorbell himself. She let him out and in about three times that day, and each time he did it. Now if anyone comes to the house she shows him off. Mrs. Jerome, the neighbour woman who drives us to church, came by twice just to watch.

I have to admit, Bronson is clever. I even have to admit that Margie's pretty smart too.

That smudge on the page, by the way, was me trying to draw Bronson at the front door, pushing the doorbell. Unfortunately Bronson looked more like a big mouse than a dog, so I rubbed it out. That's one career I won't have, Alex, the Artist.

I forgot to tell you. Last Monday Mom drove Tobey to the hospital in the city for more tests. She said the doctors poked and prodded his belly. Tobey didn't say much, but she could tell he was uncomfortable. Even though Tobey's five, he's back in diapers. I don't know why. Is it the cancer? Is it nerves? Does he want to be a baby again? They say you do that when things are scary.

I remember when Tobey was born, Margie started to wet her bed again. Mom never said a thing, and the accidents (as Mom called them) eventually stopped. She said Margie was jealous of the baby and wanted Mom for herself. Or maybe it was just because of the big changes in the house. When I think about big changes, like the beginning of a school year—especially next year when I have to go to high school—I get nervous too. I get the feeling that I'd like to be small again. Not wet my bed, of course, but to have things stay where they are familiar.

Anyway, Mom said the doctor did a scan. Poor Tobe. She said the scan machine is like a humungous donut. Tobey was velcroed onto a narrow bed which moved inside the donut hole. Tobey cried. It must be scary when you can't see. To keep him quiet and not wriggly, she held his hand and bribed him with singing. She said she sang all of Raffi's and Fred Penner's songs three times through and more. I had those CDs when I was little, and Tobey and Margie still listen to them.

Mom has to go back in a few weeks to get the results. From the look on her face, I think she knows what they'll be. It's not fair. Tobey is so small.

I know in letters it's the polite thing to ask how you're doing, but since you're never going to write back is there any point in asking? Or pretending? But I like pretending.

By the way, we had our first major snowfall last night. I guess you did too. When I woke up this morning, even before I opened the curtains, I could tell. There is a quietness that comes with the snow. And a brightness.

Talk to you soon, whether you want to or not.

a

November 15

Monday after hockey practice

Hi again, Graham,
 I wrote that under the date to give you fair warning. It's about Dad again. And hockey. So you might just want to stop reading here.
 Tonight was practice night. Dad always comes when he's here on Mondays, which is just about every Monday, unfortunately.
 The coach has me in goal now, since I'm not as good a skater as the other kids. Or that's what Dad says. I actually almost like being the goalie. You have to watch every second, be on your toes. And you have to have quick reflexes. I love the feeling of jamming my mitt in the air and lunging for a shot. When I do get a save, the other guys pound my back. I like feeling part of the team. Sometimes I can't see the puck because someone's in the way and I miss. Then I feel like a loser. But those other times are just great.
 I even like the gear. All that padding, the spider-like metal web on my face. It makes me feel safe. Behind all that covering, I can be anyone I want. Behind the mask. Like Jacques Plante or Johnnie Bower in Uncle Peter's scrapbook. My grandpa used to go on about them. When

I told Grandmama Martin on the phone that I was now a goalie, she couldn't stop talking about Ken Dryden as if he was still in the net. Behind my mask and the heavy chest and leg pads, I feel twice as strong. No one can hurt me.

Today, though, I don't know why, I was off. There was shooting practice. Sometimes Dad is wandering around, talking to adults, ignoring me. But I could hear him yelling non-stop. "How could you miss that? What a gift. Ah, dumb move." Partly it's because in shooting practice I'm the focus the whole time. There's no break for me, so there's no break in his yelling. Before I was in goal, I rarely touched the puck, so the yelling was mostly in the car coming home. Today it was all the time, and he just worked himself up more and more.

When shooting practice was over, we skated to the side so the coach could talk to us. But Dad still kept at me. "Alex, you got to be quicker. Keep your eyes on the puck. Don't be such a slacker."

"Yeah, Dad."

Then Brendan's dad, Mr. McGuire, said, "Quit it, Howard. You're not the coach. He did just fine. Have you ever had a dozen pucks flying at you all at once?" He was exaggerating about the dozen pucks. But it's true. One comes and the next, a split second after. "He did just great. I think he'll be a fantastic goalie."

Dad's face got red. "So your Brendan's such a great hockey player, is he? How many goals has he got? None, I bet. You got to push them if they're going to succeed. You can't let them be lazy and good-for-nothing. Don't you want them to win?"

"Howard, it's not about winning. It's about playing as

a team. It's about having fun. It's about getting fit."

"What crap, George. Life's not like that. No wonder your kid sucks." Now Mr. McGuire's face turned red too. Some other moms and dads were closing in.

Brendan's mom pulled his dad's sleeve. "Come on, George. Let's go for a walk. There's still half an hour of practice left."

As Mr. McGuire turned, his eyes swept over me. I'm sure I saw sympathy. Maybe I could talk to him about Dad or hang out with Brendan. He's younger than me, but the McGuires do live in town, not far from the high school. On second thought, probably not. As if he'd want to talk to me after what my dad just said about him.

You know, it's all so embarrassing, with Dad, I mean. All the neat stuff I was feeling about being goalie went up in the hot air of his anger. The other kids didn't say a word. Not a word to me during the rest of practice, not a word in the locker room. And when the dads came in after practice, he was still going on about the same stuff. I just wanted to tell him to shut up or stuff it or something. One day I will.

And do you know what was even worse? When I got home, Mom was mad at me for forgetting to take dinner out of the freezer this morning. She had to stay overnight at the hospital with Tobey, and I'd promised I'd take the chicken out. We ended up having eggs on toast, but still she was mad.

Not in the best of moods now. Hockey always brings out the worst in Dad.

Alex

19.11

D.G.

I thought I'd write no more than once a week. It doesn't seem to work out that way, does it?

Lots of times I think it would be good to live in town and not have to take the bus. I could walk to school and even come home for lunch. Other times, I like the bus. I usually sit about halfway down the aisle, right at the window, and squish my nose up, staring out at the maple trees, cows and munching sheep as they pass. I sometimes think of what I'm going to write you about when I get home. I daydream. Other times I even sing in my head. I like "Tears in Heaven" by Eric Clapton I'm trying to teach myself the chords on Uncle Peter's old acoustic guitar. I'm working on one by Oasis too.

Anyways, this morning I was in the middle of daydreaming when the school bus rumbled to a stop near the McIntyres to let kids on. When Jordan McIntyre passed me, he whacked me on the back and grabbed my toque. Then he threw it to Jeff, who threw it to Mitchell, then over to Jordan again. They tossed my hat back and forth all around the bus. I only got it back when they sent it into a bunch of girls.

I should have punched Jordan out then and there and

taken his mp3 player. Or said something smart. Instead I just grinned like a dummie. I didn't even chase after the stupid toque. Probably in the middle of the night I'll think up some perfect comment. But I never have one when I need it.

Margie was sitting two rows ahead of me and saw the whole thing. "Why are you letting them do that to you?" she said. I don't think she was being funny, but the kids laughed.

Maybe I should stop telling you junk like this. Pretty soon you'll start thinking about me like all the others do. I couldn't stand that.

Alex

Sunday, November 21

Dear Graham,

I forgot to tell you something else. I'm a little ashamed. Only a little. But maybe it proves I am a coward.

There's a new guy in our class. He's been here for a few weeks now. His name is Bennie Tran. He's quiet and is already being picked on. That's sort of good for me as I'm less the butt of Jeff's dumb jokes.

Today, it was something about "Chinky Chinky Chinaman" to Bennie. First off, he's Canadian. Like, he was born here. And second, he's not even Chinese. He told me the other day that his parents came from Vietnam, and I think he even speaks Vietnamese. Which is kind of neat—to speak another language. I wish Mom had spoken to us in French when we were little. Then I'd be at the top in French class.

Last week they did something really horrible. Jeff put dog poo in a small brown paper bag and gave it to Bennie like a present. Bennie opened it up, although I could tell he was a little wary. Then Alan pushed the bag so it was almost in his face. His face clouded, in that hurt, deflated sort of way. I knew how he felt.

I should at least have gone over and said something to him. But I stayed in the corner, out of the way. In fact, if I'm honest, I was sort of happy. Not really happy. Just relieved it wasn't me. But I should've stuck up for him.

The worst of it is, I think I like Bennie. He's quiet, as I said, and I saw him with some neat books from the library today. Anyways, gotta run. Tobey's banging on my door.

Alex, the Coward

p.s. Mom made pizza for supper. Tobey and Margie and I put our favourite stuff on our own pizzas. For me, that means mushrooms and onions and lots of cheese. Tobey likes broccoli. Can you imagine?

November 23

Dear G

It's Tuesday. I'm always glad when Tuesday comes, because Dad's gone. As soon as he leaves, it's like I can breathe again. When he's here, it's like I have this wire mesh around me, and each day the wire cranks tighter and tighter. You know what? I do think I want to be a writer when I grow up. Maybe I could write books, then someone would buy the film rights, and I'd make zillions of dollars. Then, of course, I'd write the screenplay, direct all the actors and maybe even act in it myself. So that way I could be an actor and a director.

Hey, if I'm going to dream, I might as well dream big.

...later

I forgot to tell you that Mom went back to the big hospital with Tobey yesterday. She sat us down last night after Tobey was in bed and told us about the tests. Dad was there too, which was unusual. Normally he's up in his room or watching TV. According to Mom, the doctors say Tobey's very, very sick. Dad looked upset and said "I hope your mother is exaggerating." But I'm pretty sure this was just another of his "miracle cure" lines.

Mom talked slowly. She seemed to choose each word,

probably trying to be gentle. I guess because of Margie. "The doctors showed me the scan. There are little dots of cancer spread all over his body, in his bones everywhere—head, legs, wrists. And it's growing again in his abdominal cavity."

"What's an abomnible cavity, Mom?" Margie said.

"Ab-dom-in-al." Mom patted her belly. "Inside here."

I didn't think Margie understood much. She just jumped down from the couch and ran upstairs to bed after we'd finished talking. Later I had to tiptoe into her room to get something for Mom, and there she was in bed, curled up with her thumb in her mouth. She hasn't sucked her thumb in years.

Which reminds me. Bennie was teased again at school today. He lives right in Whistler's Corners, so he walks home. Today, for some reason he was walking past our bus line-up as kids were filing on. Someone stuck out a leg on purpose and tripped him. Margie saw it and rushed over to pick up his stuff from the snow.

His backpack must've been half open because books scattered everywhere. One even went under the bus. I didn't want to climb under. But, with Margie helping him, the others laughing, Bennie wiping snow off himself and all his junk, I figured I had to. So I reached under the bus and got it. I had visions of someone booting me in the bum, the bus moving forward and me getting ground to relish. Why do I always think of the worst things happening?

I'll write again soon.

Your friend, Alex

Nov. 24

Dear Graham,

I've decided to change my name. If I had a different name, maybe I'd be a different person. Maybe I'd be strong and intelligent. Maybe all the kids would like me. Maybe I wouldn't be picked on. Maybe even Dad would like me.

So I'm going to be Mac. My whole name is Alexander Martin (that's my Mom's last name—with the accent on the second syllable) Crispin. If you switch the initials around, you get Mac. So how about that? Mac Crispin, my new name.

Cheers,
Mac

Sunday, November 28

Dear Graham,

I like writing on weekends and Mondays, because it gives me something to do in my room so I'm out of Dad's way. It's the middle of the afternoon, but Tobey's sleeping in his bed across from mine. When he was little he used to sleep a lot. Then he stopped. Lately he's gone back to having afternoon naps. Maybe senior kindergarten's tiring him out. But today is Sunday. I probably should wake him up, or he won't sleep tonight, but I like the peace and quiet with him out of the road. Plus that's Mom's job, not mine.

I really like our bedroom, actually. It's pretty cold in winter because it used to be an upstairs porch and doesn't have much insulation. It has lots of windows and lots of light, and the window frames are painted deep blue, my favourite colour. We can see in three directions, and in the winter we get the sun most of the day coming in at the sides and back. But when it's cloudy, that's when it's really cold. The other downside is we only have half a wall for posters. But hey, I still think it's the best room in the house.

The room is mainly full of Tobey's junk—blocks and books and CDs. I have a desk in the corner, but I usually do homework on the dining room table, because by the time I get around to doing it, Tobey's supposed to be sleeping. If I have to use the computer for a project or something, I go to Mom and Dad's room—but only when Dad's away. I have to be organized about that.

Grandma Crispin fell and hurt her hip yesterday when she was shopping, so Mom spent most of Saturday in Emerg with her. We don't have a hospital in Whistler's Corners, so they had to go to Davenport. This meant that Mom was away all day, and I was stuck with the two littlies—that's what I call them. I make it sound like it's a bad thing, but actually it was lots of fun.

Most of the time we tobogganed. We have a field with a super hill. The neighbours keep sheep there in the spring and summer, but it's all ours at this time of the year. We have a huge old tin toboggan that flies like you can't imagine. About the only thing we have to avoid is a telephone pole right in the middle.

Up and down, up and down we went. Between his usual fits of laughter, Tobey yelled, "One more time. One more time." My legs are still tired from it all. Margie would zip down the hill on her flying saucer and run back up twice by the time I collected Tobey and the toboggan. Sometimes we'd all slide together, Margie in the front, me at the back with Tobey between my legs. Margie got most of the snow in her face, but she never complained, just wiped it off with her mitts—or mine if she'd grabbed them off me.

When Mom got home, she looked sort of faded. But we surprised her and had dinner all ready. We made lamb chops with mashed potatoes and peas, her favourite. She gave us big, big hugs.

It looks like Grandma will have to lie around for a while to let her hip heal, so Mom is borrowing her car so she can go into town to help. Usually Mom's stuck out here in the country all week and can only go in when Dad's home. I think she's like me, though, and doesn't really have any friends—except for Mrs. Jerome who takes her to church. And I'm not sure that Mrs. Jerome is a good friend. You know what I mean. Not the kind you can talk to, like you.

Bye for now, friend.

Alex

p.s. It's Thursday now, and I'll add a few lines. I've decided Jeff and Alan are totally pathetic and some of the others too. Do you know they teased Tobey today? They're thirteen and he's only five. They called him "cross-eyes" and "baldy". Some of the other kids laughed.

Tobey does look weird, because with his blindness he seems to stare off in all different directions. But really he's trying to see out of the corner of his eyes. Fortunately, he doesn't know he looks funny, and I don't think he realizes the kids are teasing him. But I do, and it bothers me. Teasing *me* is one thing. Teasing Tobey is another.

When Jeff and Alan started picking on Tobey today, I jumped up and ran forward on the bus, intending to sit beside him. Mrs. Quinn, the driver, yelled, "Sit the heck down." Which I did. I jammed myself in the first seat I saw and wound up with two Grade Three girls and everyone laughed because the girls went "yuck" in unison. Then I crawled on the floor to get to Tobey's seat and Mrs.

Quinn got even madder. But I didn't care because it was actually fun. And by the time I got to Tobey he was laughing so hard my ears hurt. *7715*

I'm glad I stuck up for Tobey.

Mac (sort of)

Skaha Lake Middle School Library

December 6

Dear Graham,

Today we had creative writing in English. Normally I like it. This time we had to write about something special from a past Christmas. Crap, I thought, or worse than crap. I generally don't like Christmas. All the tension in our house seems to be worse at this time of year. And I knew that this wasn't the kind of thing the teacher wanted. So what to do? Make up something sappy and happy?

Yes, we have our stockings and stuff, but everyone's so irritable. Mom spends weeks baking and baking and gets annoyed if the cookies don't turn out perfect. And Dad complains if things are not to his liking. To be honest, I don't see why she makes all the cookies anyway. She says it's in case people drop in, but no one ever does other than the Lopateckis on Christmas Eve. She even makes Christmas cake in September and hides it. She says that way it ages, but I don't think that's the real reason. I think she hides it so Dad doesn't eat it all before Christmas.

We open our stockings and presents then go to Grandma Crispin's for the day. That part is pure boring. Grandma has a turkey and exactly the same thing every year. I really don't like her bread stuffing, which just comes out of a box and has a weird flavour. She doesn't make cranberries, which I like, and she makes Brussels sprouts all mushy and kind of gross. In fact, she doesn't make anything with much flavour. See what I mean? Even the food is boring.

The only good part is that I know I still have another turkey dinner to eat, because Mom cooks a turkey at New Year's. She makes stuffing, with lots of raisins and nuts, and yams in maple syrup. And if she does do Brussels sprouts, she drenches them in a cheese sauce. That way they're edible. Mainly because I like cheese.

Hey, I just got an idea for my creative writing project! I can write about the day I discovered there was no Santa Claus who flies around on a sleigh, slipping in through chimneys, eating milk and cookies and giving out presents.

If it turns out all right, and IF the teacher likes it, I'll show you. Maybe. Okay?

Alex (Ooops)
Mac

p.s. Sometimes I wonder why I don't just write a journal. But I don't think it would be the same. I like to imagine you're glad to see the envelope in the hall when you get home from school. You rip it open, shove it between your teeth as you take off your jacket and start reading halfway up the stairs to your bedroom.

December 10

Hi G,

You would be proud of me this morning. Actually, I'm proud of myself. As usual Tobey was sitting in the front seat of the bus with another little boy. He'd taken off his toque and was sitting quietly. The kindergarten kids always sit in the front rows, and Tobey's now right opposite the driver because of his blindness. Same spot, so he doesn't get confused and all that. Mrs. Quinn, the driver, lets us bigger kids off first then goes round the corner of the school to let the littlies off separately.

As we were shuffling past, Jeff "the bully" Pinsent hissed, "Hey, elephant ears." When Tobey had a mop of red hair, you never noticed his ears. Now with his short layer of fuzz, you see them. And they do stick out—but just a little.

The next thing, Jeff's hand shot out and tweaked poor, defenseless Tobey's left ear. Tobey yelped, looked around in that funny way he has, and put his head down. The other littlies called out, "Mrs. Quinn, Tobey's hurt."

Mrs. Quinn couldn't see anything because of the big kids filing past. But I saw. I was about four behind Jeff. Outside the bus, I grabbed his shoulder and said, "I guess you must feel really bad about your own humungous sticky-outy ears when you have to pick on a five-year-old who's blind and sick with cancer." I kept walking. My heart pounded so loudly I thought the whole world could hear it. I just barrelled on, thinking he would come up behind and punch me out. Nothing.

He'll get me later, I'm sure of that. But it was worth it. You know, sometimes I feel ashamed that I'm picked on. But today, for the first time, I thought he's the one who should be ashamed. Today I'm definitely,

Mac

p.s. I've been extra busy lately watching the littlies after school and even making supper (easy stuff like hamburgers) because Mom has to take Grandma to the doctor and help her buy food and Christmas presents. I wonder if we'll still go to her house on Christmas. It would be nice to be home. And probably easier. No schlepping of us kids and food into town.

Don't you like that word? Schlepping? I don't even know if that's the right spelling. I heard someone use it the other day on the radio—they were talking about carrying a lot of heavy musical instruments around, but I think that sounds good for kids too.

p.p.s. I nearly forgot. At noon Bennie came up to me. "I hear you got Jeff really good," he said. I was so shocked all I could do was mumble, "Thanks." Someone must have seen and heard and talked. Nice of Bennie, eh?

p.p.p.s. Crap. It's after nine, and I haven't started my math homework.

December 13, Tuesday

G,

Argh, I get so annoyed. Mom's always on at me to do more around the house. But Dad does nothing. Is it the same at your place? I already do more than he does, watching Margie and Tobey after school most days. If Dad doesn't do anything, why should I? What's the difference? Mom says, "Oh, he works hard and he's tired. I can't bother him." Maybe she doesn't consider school real work.

And not only is Dad no help, he never stops criticizing Mom. Last night he complained that we only had cookies and canned peaches for dessert. Poor baby. "Honestly, Julie, why can't you make a decent dessert? You don't work. The least you can do is bake." Mom's in town looking after *your* mother is what I wanted to say, but didn't.

Mom's hair was pulled back in a ponytail. I could see her ears get red. I wish she'd say something, but she doesn't. Maybe she's afraid of him. Or afraid she'll say what she really and truly thinks, then regret it. Like me.

Like Saturday night. It was the annual Christmas hockey banquet. All the dads go with their sons, although there are a few girls who play and bring their dads too. It's kind of strange that more girls don't play. I bet Margie would be great. She loves skating. She goes like the wind at everything, especially sporty things. I wonder what

Dad would think. Then again he'd probably just say she's a better hockey player than me. Actually, I wouldn't care because I think she'd be good, even very good. Like another Hayley Wickenheiser. If I had to choose a sport for me, it'd be running or cross-country skiing.

Back to the Christmas hockey banquet. It was in at the Legion, and we had roast beef and veggies and, of course, apple and lemon pies. As usual Dad talked about what great research he's doing these days, how important he is. He never asks how the other person is. It's always about him. You can see the other faces at the table go sort of blank eventually. It's embarrassing.

They gave out a few awards—not a lot of them like at the end of the season. The most improved this and the best that. Of course I didn't get one, and Dad reminded me all the way home. "You should get one for the least improved player," he even said. I could feel my face burn and was all ready to say, "Yeah and you should get one for the mouthiest father." But I didn't. I would have been mushed apple. Mushed Mac apple. Yuck. Yuck.

Bye for now from

Not mushed Mac. Or is it Alex?

December 16

Dear G,

Yesterday after school, Margie and I decided to make some gingerbread as a treat for Mom. She was upstairs reading to Tobey. We figured gingerbread would be easy and we all love it warm with hot applesauce poured over it.

We found the recipe in her old—like I mean ancient—Five Roses Cook Book. The book's all in pieces with the index half gone, but we found it. Actually, we nearly missed it. For some dumb reason gingerbread is under P for prize gingerbread and not under G.

We had lots of fun. We put the flour and baking powder in one bowl then got out another bowl, the way the recipe said, for the butter, brown sugar, eggs, molasses and hot water. I've probably missed some ingredients, but you get the picture.

"What's that racket?" Mom called down, when we started the electric mixer, beating the floury stuff into the runny stuff. "What are you guys up to?"

I ran to the bottom of the stairs and yelled, "Don't worry, Mom. We're making a surprise for you."

In that five seconds, Margie lifted the beaters out of the batter. And, yup, you guessed it. By the time I got back there were bits of brown, uncooked gingerbread glops on the walls, the cupboards, the fridge, the windowpane, the floor, Margie's face and shirt and even her hair. I yanked the cord out of the wall. I was ready to yank her arms out of their sockets too.

But I had to laugh. Fortunately so did Mom. "You guys certainly did make a surprise for me." There was Margie slurping up the goop on the ends of her hair. I'm sure it will be next week before we find all the batter splatters (hey, I like those words).

a.

December 19

Dear Graham,

I hope you're not getting tired of all these letters? What do you do with them? If you were sending them to me, I would keep them in a shoe box up on the top shelf of my cupboard. Then I could go back and read them again and again.

You probably got that same big dump of snow we got last night. Tobey and Margie and I spent half the afternoon building snowpeople. First we made one big snowman, but we ended up making a whole snow family—we even found stones in the corner of the garage to make eyes and mouths. Tobe really got into it. We pushed and rolled and patted until I was cold, my mitts were soggy and all our scarves and hats were on the snowpeople. By the end of it, Tobey was tripping over himself from tiredness. Bronson ran around, tail whisking back and forth, barking at the snowpeople and getting in our way. When we finally went in, Mom had apple cider on the stove the way I like it, heated up and cinnamon-y. This is when I think being in the country can be good.

School is out. I'm sure you're happy. I'm not so sure I am. I wonder what you're doing for the holidays. And Bennie.

Cheers,
Mac

December 24

Dear Graham,

I should have wished you Merry Christmas with my last letter because this one won't get to you in time. I will now, so....Merry Christmas.

Dad picked up a tree for us in town last weekend. Me, I sort of like the scrawny ones, the ones that are left over. Do you ever wonder what it must be like not to be chosen as a tree? It reminds me of being the last one chosen for a team in gym. But this Christmas tree is almost perfect, although Dad did complain there weren't many decent ones left.

We always decorate the tree on the 21st, because it's the longest night. This year we had a great time. In the afternoon Tobey, Mom and I strung paper chains and popcorn. Mom says she did that when she was little, and we're carrying on a tradition. Mom did the stringing and Tobey the popcorn eating and me a bit of both. Margie was at her friend Jasmine's, so she missed out.

After supper, Mom got Tobey and Margie into their pjs, and I got out all the cardboard boxes full of decorations. Mom put on some Christmas CDs, and Tobey danced around the living room. Every year we decorate the tree the same way, starting with the lights. Then one at a time we choose a decoration and carefully place it on a branch. It takes forever and we have shortbread and

Christmas cake and ooh and ahh over our favourite ornaments. Mom tells us where each of the decorations came from—not that I can remember most of it, except the red ball with tiny shiny beads down the side from my great-grandmama. And then there are a bunch that were made by my aunts for each of us when we were babies. Mom says the ones with our names on them will go to us when we are big and have trees of our own.

Although Tobey can't see much, he got to put decorations on too. We left the bottom-most branches for him, the middle bits for Margie, and Mom and I shared the top. The angel goes on last. We take turns to put her on too. This was Tobey's year. I lifted him up by his legs. When I tried to hold him around the waist, he yelped. His belly hurts more than I realized. Mom guided his hands to the top of the tree. As he placed the angel on top, Margie plugged in the lights. There was a hush. Then we curled up together in a big jumble on the couch, feeling the magic.

Even though it was Tuesday, Dad was at home. He's taken vacation until the New Year. As usual he was upstairs doing more important things, like working on one of his papers for a biology conference or something. To be honest, I preferred it that way. When he heard our oohs and aahhs, he came down to see. You know, he can't just once say, "Wow, that looks fantastic. You've done a great job." Nope. He just starts moving stuff, saying "There are too many candy canes on this side" or "Why didn't you buy more icicles?" Little things. It's like he wants to prick our balloon of fun. This year, Mom ignored it. She smiled and shooed the little ones off to bed. I decided he couldn't spoil my evening either.

I was wondering, when Dad's so down on things, what fun he has, if ever. Come to think of it, does Dad ever laugh except a sort of ha-ha at his own dumb put-down jokes? I can almost feel sorry for him.

I do complain a lot about Dad and even school. But I am lucky. Margie, Mom, Tobey and I have lots of great times together. Like Tuesday night when we put up the tree.

And tonight. It was really special too.

Often on Christmas Eve we go to the candlelight service at church. That's about the only time I enjoy going, because we do lots of singing and get to hold candles. The whole church is dark except for the flickering lights. It's so peaceful.

But for some reason we didn't go this year. So after the Lopateckis left, Margie and I thought it would be fun to light our own candles. We gathered all we could find and placed them outside in the snow bank, around and in front of the house. Then we lit them one at a time. I think Tobey could see the lights because he sighed as each one caught fire. But the best time was after they were all lit. Mom came out and for a few minutes we just stood huddled together watching the light. Even Margie was quiet.

Afterwards Bronson bounded out, sticking his nose into each of the snow holes. He jumped away when he singed his whiskers then went straight to the next one and did it all over again. We laughed. And we thought he was smart! Oh well.

Merry Christmas,
a.

31 December

Dear G,

I think I told you I don't usually enjoy the Christmas holidays. You must think I was lying, because this year I'd just been telling you about good times. Maybe I'm not letting Dad bug me the way I used to. Plus I try not to tell you about the other times.

On Wednesday Tobey had an appointment at the hospital in the city again. It was the first time I'd been to the clinic. It was kind of nice to be there because it's sort of like Tobey's place. He seemed right at home. Despite his bad eyes, he showed Margie and me where all the toys are kept, and we played on the floor until he and Mom had to see Dr. Pilecki. Mom didn't say anything afterwards except that Tobey has to go back for more tests. All they ever do is tests, tests, tests. My sense is things are getting worse, although Mom doesn't say much, and I don't ask. Mom looks smaller and sort of pinched in.

Afterwards we all went to the Science Centre. Tobey and Margie pushed every button possible, and I tried to make sense of the astronomy stuff to impress Dad. Margie chattered, and Tobey slept all the way home. Mom was very quiet.

I have a secret to tell you. This morning Mom made tourtières for supper and two mincemeat pies for New

Year's Day. She placed them on the counter while the oven was heating up and we did the dishes. Her hands were in the sink and mine wrapped around a plate when we heard a noise. We both turned. There was Bronson wiping the crust of each pie with his long pink tongue. Mom looked at me. I looked at Mom. "We didn't see that, did we, Alex?" Each word came out of her mouth very slowly.

"See what?" I replied. She popped the pies into the oven, and we both burst out laughing.

I got a really nice stereo system from my dad for Christmas, by the way. It's large, with big speakers, and right after we finished opening presents, Dad came up to my room and hooked it up. The only part I didn't like was that he took my old one. He didn't ask me or anything. He just took it and put it straight in Margie's room. I wouldn't have kept two. I would have given it to Margie. But he didn't let me do it. Still, I'm happy with the new system.

By the way, Mom has a black eye and a bruise on the side of her cheek. She told me she ran into the bathroom door upstairs.

I looked straight at her and said, "Yeah, right." She knew I knew. I don't like that she lied to me.

Happy New Year, Graham. I mean it. I really, really hope we both have a good one.

Mac

January 2

Dear Gray,

New Year's Day was very cold. All morning, Mom of course was doing the turkey, the stuffing and the veggies. Margie wanted to go out, but I didn't want to freeze as she ran in circles, so I suggested we put on a play for Mom, Dad, Grandma, and Uncle Peter and Aunt Marion who were visiting us from Toronto. We got one of Margie's old story books called *There's No Such Thing as a Dragon*. She bought it for five cents at a garage sale years ago. It's all tattered. But she still likes reading it, especially to Tobey.

We had to change it around a whole lot. Tobey got to be the Mom, because all he had to say was "There's no such thing as a dragon." Margie of course had to be the dragon. I was the narrator and general organizer.

We practised it all morning. We had Tobey dressed in an apron. He just roared around saying over and over, "There's no such thing as a dragon," pretending to vacuum, pretending to serve dinner. I'm always amazed how well he gets around, despite being blind.

Margie's costume was more complicated. In the story the dragon grows bigger and bigger the more he's ignored. We tied together sweaters and scarves to make dragon-extensions so that Margie-the-dragon could grow and grow. All this pretty much took up the rest of the day.

For supper we had turkey and our usual yummy yams (that's my name for them because of all the maple syrup Mom puts in them) and red cabbage with lots of apples. It was really good, except that Uncle Peter and Dad fought all through dinner, which is pretty normal for them. I think that's the reason we don't see much of him and Aunt Marion.

After dinner we went to the living room and performed the play. Everyone clapped and laughed uproariously. Even Dad seemed to be enjoying himself, although Grandma had to keep shushing him because he kept making remarks.

I think I'm going to call Dad the dragon in the house. I wonder if it's the same thing. The more we don't talk about what he's like and the more he gets his own way, the bigger a dragon he gets.

I forgot to tell you—we did go to Grandma's for Christmas dinner. Dad got his way as usual. And Mom, as usual, didn't stand up for herself. When she asked him to help set the table, he refused. Even Grandma suggested he help, because she gets tired quickly, but he just lounged around and watched TV. Mom did all the food preparation, and I looked after the littlies. We went out and made snow angels and played board games in the spare bedroom. It was okay.

Why doesn't Mom ever stand up for herself? Why does Grandma mostly give in to him too? Dad, I mean.

Talk to you soon,

Alex

January 6

Dear G,

I just had to write today because of what happened in English class. Hold your breath. Wait for it. Here it comes.....Tah Dum!! Mrs. Mayo really liked my creative writing piece. I can't believe it. She really, really liked it. I got an A+, something I've never gotten in my whole life for anything. After class she asked me to stay for a minute. I figured she must have changed her mind about my grade or something.

But then she said, "Alex, do you like writing stories?"

I just gulped and nodded. "I read a lot. But I've never written much."

"You should do more of it," she said. "I mean it. That story of yours is one of the best-written stories I've ever had from one of my students. You have a gift."

"You mean to be a writer?" I'm sure I blushed, and was very glad none of the kids were around to hear what she said. I have a gift. To be a writer. Yeah, right.

She nodded. And then—this will blow your socks off—she said "Are you trying out for the play? Auditions are on the 25th. I really think you should." I just hung there in the air like an old cloth bag, blown back and forth by her suggestion.

Finally, I said, "I don't know if I could. I mean, I don't

even know what you do in an audition."

She smiled. She has eyes that sometimes look green, sometimes look blue. Today they were green. "Not to worry. Nobody else does either." She grinned back at me. I know I must have looked relieved. "Find a piece of poetry or story you really like and memorize it. Learn it with expression and emphasis, as if it's real."

"But what could I use?"

"Anything. Anything you like. You could use what you've written yourself. Or a poem can be easier to memorize, especially if it rhymes. Or, what about something we studied this year, like from *Romeo and Juliet*?"

My mind raced. One moment I thought I could do it. After all, I did it for my family only last week. The next I remembered how nervous I get answering questions in class, let alone speaking in front of the whole school and half the town. But Mrs. Mayo just stood there looking at me.

"Don't worry, you'll be great. If you have any questions, please come and ask." I could tell she was wanting me to leave. My head was spinning so hard, I needed to get out of there too.

So what do you think? Should I? Should I do something fancy from Shakespeare or perform my silly story? I think I'll print off a copy and send it to you, although you won't get to read where Mrs. Mayo scrawled *"Great work!! I really loved it!"* across the bottom.

Mac

I burst into the hall. A wave of heat washed over me. I kicked off my snow boots on the linoleum tile, tossed my mittens on the radiator and hopped over the pools of water. The mittens sizzled. Ribbons of cards draped the door frame.

My ears tingled, listening hard for people sounds.

In the living room, I could see icy scribbles on the windowpanes. The brown sofa, shifted over near the tall, standing lamp, made room for a fir tree, sparkly green and silent in the corner. An angel smiled on top.

I tiptoed up the stairs and pushed open the varnished door to my parents' bedroom, the knob cool to touch. Cccrreeeek. My eardrums thumped. The curtains were half-closed. But I could see the dresser, strewn with bobby pins, combs, lipstick and puffs of Kleenex. A shiny hairbrush glinted on the propped-up photo of my New Brunswick grandmama.

I listened harder. My snowpants swished, swished. No sounds of laughter. No doors slamming. The radiator gurgled.

I'm six and I can read and print and sing. Why do they shshhsh and say I'm too little to understand? Why can't I know things that big people know?

I slid across the bumpy waxed floor in my sock feet. The bed loomed large, not a wrinkle in the spread. Underneath, behind that forbidden curtain of fringed edges was where I knew Mom kept them. The Christmas presents.

I wiggled my bulky form under the bed until my fingers nudged a mound of slippery, uncrinkled paper. I pulled it out. I flopped the red parcel over. No scotch tape. It rolled and unrolled into a toque with matching mittens and a label: "To Alex, From Santa". In my mother's handwriting.

My head swooshed. My ears clanged.

A sudden cool breath of air hit me. Someone had opened the front door. I gave the present one quick shove under the bed and ran. In the bathroom I unzipped my jacket, pulled down my snow pants and sat. And sat. My heart and head thudded.

"Alex. Where are you?"

"Upstairs. In the bathroom."

Now I knew things about Santa other kids didn't know. Maybe not things I wanted to know. I also knew I couldn't tell anyone.

Maybe I had just become big.

January 10

Dear Graham,

As usual I'm writing after school in my room. It's really cold here today—outside it's minus 25, and inside it doesn't feel much better. That's an exaggeration, but it still means I've tucked my duvet all around my knees and toes. If my writing is worse than usual, it's because I've got gloves on too.

Today at school Alan Bertuzzi stole my lunch and danced around the room. When the teacher came back Bennie Tran told her, but of course the bag was in the garbage by then with other half-finished lunches on top. Even though the teacher made Alan get it, I sure didn't feel like eating it.

I didn't see it, but one of the girls told me that Jeffrey jumped Bennie for telling on Alan. They shoved his face into the snowbank and scraped it back and forth a whole bunch of times. By the end of the day, it still had a red, raw look. After school I said "Thanks" and "Sorry about your face." Bennie only nodded. Then I asked if he'd like me to tell Mrs. Mayo or the principal about it. He shook his head, but smiled a we'll-get-them-one-day smile.

Mac or Alex (I'm not sure who)

January 13

Dear G,

Today for a change I had no littlies to look after when I got home, so I went cross country skiing. The snow was crisp and white with long shadows. I made my own path over the back field but had to watch for the big hunks of rock that Dad says are part of the Canadian Shield— they can really crunch your skis if you're not careful. It was beautiful, the sun glinting through the pine and hemlock trees. I like being by myself, I like the quiet and the squeak of snow under my skis and even the bite of cold in my face.

I have a hockey game tomorrow night. It's early. I hope Dad's not home in time. I definitely like hockey better since I've been playing in goal. But I prefer skiing, and I think I'd like to jog in the summer. I can do them on my own, and there's no big deal about winning or losing.

Then again, I could try karate and maybe kick Jeffrey Pinsent you know where, and he'd never bother me again.

Mac—the Karate Kid—Crispin

Jan. 17

Hi G,

Hockey was fun last Friday. We beat the Davenport team four-to-one. I do love shooting my arms and legs out and sprawling on the ice. When I'm goalie, my body and brain have to be completely focussed every second. I feel super-strong behind all that padding. Maybe I should wear it all the time. (Joke)

The best part was that Dad wasn't there, and Mr. Cavanaugh drove me home. He laughed with Jim and me and even said I did a good job. I'd like to come home with them all the time.

On Sunday, we had an INCIDENT, like they say at school. Only it was at home. It was during supper. Margie was rocking back and forth on her chair. Mom told to her stop, but the next thing we knew she'd tipped over. Her head made a loud crack on the hardwood floor. In the process she broke the back of the chair.

Dad was furious. "You stupid idiot, you've broken the chair. Do you know how much that costs?" Margie was screaming. Mom cradled her in her arms on the floor. Poor Tobey was crying too, hanging onto Mom's side, probably wondering what on earth was happening. Dad just stood over them yelling, "Get up. Stop that screaming or I'll give you the walloping of your life." Meanwhile, Mom was trying to soothe Margie and Tobey and calm Dad.

Then me, Mac Crispin, super-kid in disguise, grabbed Dad by the shoulder. "Margie is hurt. Maybe she has a concussion. Do you care? Or do you just care about stupid chairs?" I don't know where the word concussion came from, but it sounded good. I was shaking, I was so mad.

Dad got me by the wrist, but I broke free. I ran. He ran. I think he was surprised. He chased me a couple of times around the table then for some reason I took off through the living room and out the front door into the snow. I had no jacket, just my big fleece on and my old running shoes. Dad stopped almost immediately. I headed toward Lopatecki's barn but circled back and around after about five minutes because I was freezing. But when I returned the front door was locked. I knew my dad had done it on purpose.

I slipped around to the back and found the door there unlocked. During the winter it's usually kept locked, because going in and out that way lets in too much cold air. Mom must have pulled the bolt, knowing what Dad had done.

When I came in, Dad was already watching television in the living room. I tiptoed upstairs and found Mom in Margie's room, Margie still whimpering. Tobey was lying on her bed, pretending to read a book to her. Mom looked me straight in the eye with a fierceness I've never seen before and said, "Your dad locked that door, Alex. That's unacceptable. I'm sorry."

I wanted to say, "Let's leave."

Your friend, Mac

January 20

Dear Graham,

The auditions for the school play are next week. Do I have the nerve? Every night I've been memorizing a short bit from *Romeo and Juliet* where Romeo says,

But, soft! What light through yonder window breaks?
It is the east, and Juliet is the sun!
Arise, fair sun, and kill the envious moon,
Who is already sick and pale with grief,
That thou, her maid, art far more fair than she.

I just say it over and over until I go to sleep. I know those words now. I may add a few more lines. Plus I have to put real meaning into it. I went to Mrs. Mayo and asked her what the lines meant—to be sure. That helped.

She said she was pleased I was practising but had noticed I hadn't actually put my name down on the audition list at the back of the room. There are slots for names and times. I said I would. But I'm not sure, really. I do want to, though.

Today in class Jeff called Bennie "Chinkie Chinkie" again. I don't know what got into me, but I leaned around and singsonged back, "Dinkie Dinkie". All the other guys cracked up. Even if Jeff gets me, those guys laughing with me was worth it.

Tobey didn't go to school this week. He's sleeping a lot more in the afternoons now and even some in the mornings, Mom says.

Alex

25th of January

Dear Graham,

I did it. The audition, I mean. I can't believe it, but I did.

All day today I was scared, scared spitless, as Mom would say. Even all last weekend, I couldn't stop thinking about it. Of course, I didn't tell anyone at home, and I particularly didn't want Dad to find out. I was so glad the auditions were being held on a day when he was away.

In class Mrs. Mayo just reminded us that auditions would be in the gym at lunch. Anyone still wanting to sign up would have to do so right after class. Each person would be called in, one at a time, and Mr. Souliere, the French teacher, and her would be the only people allowed in the room during the audition. I was relieved to hear that. As soon as the bell rang, I went to the sign-up sheet at the back of the room and put my name down in the only blank spot left—the very first space. I guess no one wanted to go first.

When I arrived at the waiting room at lunch, I was surprised to see who was trying out. Of course a lot more girls than guys were there, but almost half the class was auditioning. Lee, Garnet, Rhys, Eddie and even Jordan. I didn't know *he* would be interested. Thankfully, Alan and Jeff were nowhere to be seen.

Mr. Souliere arrived only a moment later to call me in, and I'm sure I must've gone as white as a ghost. My teeth chattered, and my feet felt like ice as we walked down the corridor together towards the gym. He showed me backstage. With a pat on the shoulder and a whispered "Break a leg", he left me all alone to walk to the front. There, far below, like in some huge pit, was Mrs. Mayo, smiling.

"What are you planning on reciting, Alex?" she said. When I reminded her, she nodded, "Ah, yes. A good choice. Go ahead when you're ready."

By this time Mr. Souliere was beside her. My stomach knotted. My mouth was dry. What was I doing here? What was the point? Why not leave right away? No words came. It felt like hours. The lines still didn't come. I cleared my throat.

"Go ahead, Alex."

I was back in my room, and Tobey was smiling at me from the corner. I would do it for Tobey. And you were there too. I spoke to both of you.

"But, soft! What light through yonder window breaks?"

It was centuries ago. I was Romeo, and you two were standing in the pits, watching, listening and cheering me on. Afterwards there were hundreds of others too, the sound of cheers ringing in my ears.

Mrs. Mayo's "Bravo" startled me. I bowed formally and walked back to the classroom with Mr. Souliere. I was glad I had gone first, that it was over, especially when I saw the scared look on most of the other kids' faces. And, you know, I do want a part, but if I don't get one, I'm glad I tried. I'm glad I didn't wimp out.

Mrs. Mayo seemed enthusiastic about how I'd done,

but she's probably that way with everyone. She's like that. There are about nine parts for the play, so I might get something. I hope.

Keeping my fingers crossed. You too, please.

Mac, the Actor

Groundhog Day
and Margie's Birthday

Dear G,

Apparently the groundhog didn't see his shadow, so I guess spring is coming soon. Can't you just imagine Mr. Groundhog popping out of his burrow, tiny head swivelling around a couple of times taking in the weather, then muttering to himself in a deep groundhog-ee voice, "Hmmm. Looks like I've only got time for a short nap."

Now, I know you probably just think I'm stalling, not telling about the results of the auditions. But the results STILL aren't out! Now that I've actually tried out for the play I really—like really, really—want a part. I keep telling myself over and over that the important thing is I tried. The important thing is that I was able to get up in front of Mrs. Mayo and Mr. Souliere and do a half-decent job. Usually I don't try something new unless I have to, because I think I'll make a fool of myself. But maybe I'm getting some courage after all—a bit at least.

Another thing I'd like to tell you about is Bennie. Well, I guess it isn't really about Bennie. It's about me. You know, sometimes I wish you were here and we could have a really good talk. Anyways, I've told you that I get teased, and so does Bennie. It's really not just teasing.

Actually, it's more like bullying. I told Mom the other day about what the guys do to Bennie. Of course, she said that it's horrible, but I couldn't tell her they do the same to me. She asked me what I did when it happened.

"Usually nothing," I admitted. "If I tell a teacher, I'll just get into more trouble with the guys. And *you'd* better not go telling the school." I almost yelled at her. When she asked what Bennie does about it, I realized suddenly that he doesn't seem to care.

And I've thought about that a lot since. The more he ignores it, the less and less he seems to get teased. And when he does get picked on, it's more the "Chinkee Chinkee" comments and the hat snatching, not the shoving around or the-wipe-your-face-in-the-snow type of stuff. Yeah, it doesn't seem to bother him, or at least he doesn't show it. I thought it would be the other way around. I thought if I avoided Jeff and Alan and pretended to be a fly on the wall so they wouldn't see me, they'd leave me alone. But it's like the smaller I make myself, the more they like it and the more they pick on me.

What about an experiment? I'll walk around the school, slouching and sort of nervous then, another time, I'll stride around the school like I am full of confidence. I'll still be nervous, of course, but I wonder if kids would treat me differently?

In class today the guidance counsellor came in and talked about anger. She said anger was good and that you have to "release" the angry energy by putting it into action or something like that. You can just imagine the comments that came from Alan. Like, "I'm going to release my anger on your face, Crispin." Jeff wasn't there, or it would've been worse. I thought what the teacher said sounded dumb. Imagine me saying it was great my dad was hitting me. After all, he's just "releasing" his anger on me. I felt like saying how stupid could she be.

Happy Groundhog Day,

Alex

p.s. Hey, I forgot to tell you about Margie's birthday party. She had seven kids over. They tobogganed down the hill and skated on the little backyard rink Dad made for her. Mom had the party on Saturday (a few days early) so he was there. He actually came down from his home office and was nice to the kids for a change. I helped a bit with Tobey—which mostly meant reading to him on his bed. I worry about him.

February 8

Hi G,

Guess what? I got a part in the play. Not any old part, either. The main guy role!!! Can you imagine? Me? Mrs. Mayo took me aside after lunch to say I might be nervous about the idea of having such a big part (can she read my mind?), but I was not to worry. By the time the day of the play comes, she says, it'll all be great. She knows I can do it.

I'm not so sure.

Mac, the Actor

.....later

Hi again.

I didn't think I should send off such a short letter, so I'm adding on. Things are getting worse here, and me worrying about the play doesn't help. Mom's always running into town to help Grandma. And Tobey isn't up to going to school, so Mom has to drag him along. This means housework and stuff here isn't getting done, which means Dad is grumbling even more.

I heard them arguing too, Mom and Dad that is. Mom rarely raises her voice or talks back. But this time she did. "I've been looking after your mother."

"That's what women do. You're not working, so you've got lots of time." Typical Dad.

"No, I don't have lots of time, because I'm busy looking after the kids and keeping the house to your liking. Plus she's *your* mother. Why don't you help her?" Stand up to him, Mom. Good for you.

Actually, something just struck me. Tobey goes to bed really early now, so that means once he's asleep, I'll have more time in our room, if I'm pretty quiet, to practise the play. It used to be that Mom read to him, then he fooled around before going to sleep. Now he conks out right after supper.

I'm still thinking about what the guidance counsellor said. She asked what anger meant to us and whether we get angry. It may sound silly, but I never saw myself as angry. I think of Dad, of him hitting me and Mom, of his name-calling, telling us we're stupid. If that's anger, I don't have it. Plus, I don't want it. But she said anger is just an emotion, a feeling. Not actions. That blew me away. A feeling? An emotion? Maybe that isn't news to you, but it was to me. Dad is angry. But what he does, like hitting and yelling, is not anger. That's what she said. That's hitting and yelling.

I guess then it makes it okay for me to be angry. I never ever wanted to be angry like my dad. But what she said is that I can be angry, but I can decide not to hit and yell and scream. "Anger isn't the problem," she said. "The problem is that sometimes people hurt each other when they're angry instead of talking about it." The important thing is to figure out what we're really angry at and not kick the dog when we're actually mad at our teacher.

This means I should say to Dad, "Hey, Dad. I think you're angry at me. Do you want to talk about it?" Yeah, right. I asked Mom last month why Dad gets so angry at hockey. She said something about he always wanted to be a good hockey player, so since he can't be now, I have to be. But how is yelling at me when I let in a goal going to make me a better player? If he's angry, he must be angry at himself for not playing hockey. Why does he take it out on me?

It makes no sense.

I wish you could come for a visit, and we could talk about all this. We could hang out and go hiking in the fields and maybe even go winter camping. How would you like that? We could take a tent over in the bush behind the old barn and heat up some soup on our camp stove.

I could even tell you that maybe I am angry. Angry at Dad for hitting Mom.

Alex

p.s. It was my birthday on Sunday. Mom said she was too tired to make another cake. She hoped I was big enough not to mind. Not getting a birthday cake, that is. I know I'm not a kid anymore but I did mind. Kind of.

Valentine's Day

Hi Graham,

We hand out valentines at school for Valentine's Day, although the girls are more into it than the boys. Do you do it at your school? Did you get any? Someone left one for me in my desk, but I think it was one of the guys being mean. No one would give me a valentine.

Do your parents give each other valentines? Or flowers? Mine don't.

I'm living and breathing the play now. Three days a week at lunch, we work on it, and sometimes we even rehearse during school hours. Bennie's the stage manager. He smiles and talks to everyone nicely. No yelling or saying how we—or me—screwed up. I was nervous that I'd be yelled at all the time. But there's none of that, and now I'm not afraid of making a mistake. I like Bennie.

That got me to wondering why I screw up so much at home or at hockey. I think it's because I'm always afraid of making a mistake. So I do. I'm afraid mostly of what Dad will do, so I get nervous, then I really do blow it. That sounds a bit dorky, but I think it's true.

Funny, we've had only a few rehearsals of the play, but already I see things differently. Like last week when Dad heard I got a major role, he said I'd screw it up. Mom stood up for me, which was nice. But, you know, it didn't really bother me. About Dad, I mean. Before I would've said, "Yeah, he's right. I'll probably blow it. Why bother even trying?" Now sometimes I get really nervous. Sometimes I even think I'll screw up. But most times I say to myself, "I'm going to prove him wrong." I sometimes even call him names in my head. I can hear you cheering.

I was thinking some more about the anger business. I'm definitely angry at Dad for how he treats Mom. If I put my anger (as the teacher says) into action, it would mean kicking him in the face. Or somewhere even worse. Mom once told me, when the little kids were asleep, that she (and that means us too) was going to leave. I wonder if she really meant it. Because I know I couldn't ever kick Dad myself—I'd be afraid of what he'd do, and besides, that would make me just like him. But sometimes I get so angry, so so angry I want to get out of here.

Am I angry at the guys at school? Maybe I should be, but I'm not. They're just mean. Stupid too. I'm definitely angry at me for being so dorky. But really I think I'm angry at me for being such a coward, for being afraid of my father. No kid should be afraid of his dad. But I am. Sometimes I think he might hit us so hard he'd kill me or Mom.

But if I am a coward, I'm not as much as I used to be.

It's time to change the subject.

Mom's given up even suggesting Tobey should go to school. Today she came home with a small pot of crocuses and daffodils, just barely up. Mom said Tobey insisted she buy them. I know Mom would never do that on her own. She's very careful with money. Dad only lets her have a certain amount.

72

Anyways, Tobey asked over and over what bulbs were. I must have told him a dozen times until I realized he just wanted to tell *me*. So I asked, "What's a bulb, Tobey?"

"It's what happens with some plants," he said. "They go to sleep in the pot under the dirt for a while. Then in spring, they pop up and make new plants." He grabbed my face and pulled me to him, his eye almost mushed into my nose. "New flowers. They need rain and sunshine. They die. But they grow again. In different pots. They keep going. In different gardens."

I don't know why, but I felt weird. Spooked even. Like he was telling me something, I didn't know what. Tobey is so little, but sometimes he seems so old. Maybe that happens when you get sick.

a.

February 22

Dear Graham,

Last time I wrote, I thought of making a list of the things I could do to stop being a coward—like I could speak up when someone is being picked on, stick up for Mom when Dad's not treating her well, tell Dad what I think of him. You get the picture. Well, today I did one thing from my list. I was walking down the corridor, and Alan stuck out his leg to trip Bennie. I grabbed Bennie and stopped him from falling. Then I turned and gave Alan my dirtiest look and said, "How can you be such a jerk?" and walked away. I felt like the whole school was looking at me and waiting for me to get smashed in. But nothing happened.

Yet.

The best part was that Bennie asked if I'd like to go with him to karate lessons after school. I phoned Mom to say I'd be late and crossed my fingers that someone would be able to give me a ride home. You know, I thought I would like karate, and guess what? I was totally right. I really like it. It isn't a kick-the-face-out-of-the-next-person type deal like boxing. Or at least the way Mr. Saumier teaches it, it isn't. It's more about learning to focus and understanding different techniques. Actually it was him, the teacher, who drove me home afterwards. He lives way out beyond us, apparently, several lines over, meaning maybe I could go every week.

I really like Bennie. Or have I already told you that?

The play is fun. I've a lot of lines to memorize, but they seem to be coming. The problem is you just don't have to know your own lines, you have to know practically everybody else's too. Or so it seems. And you have to listen all the time. Really listen. Because you have to know what they are saying just before you say your bit. I never realized that.

Sarah, the girl who plays another main part, is always forgetting her lines. Bennie does the coaching. The hard part is that if she jumps in with the wrong line, somehow we have to say what needs to be said, even though it's in the wrong order. Mrs. Mayo's really patient when we wing the words. "Don't worry about it for now," she says. She wants us to be able to scramble our way out of a mess.

Do you know, I even have to sing a few lines. Not a real song, or a real solo (thank goodness!), but I have to sort of sing to myself. But still it's out loud. The only time I've ever sung is to Tobey and Margie or in my room with my guitar or a CD blaring. Good thing she didn't tell me at the beginning, otherwise I might never have agreed to the part.

When I'm in the play, I'm another person. It's like wussy me doesn't have to be scared, because I'm somebody else. I just magically forget about Dad, about Jeff, about being different, about being no good at anything. I'm half Harry, the character, and half Mac, the actor. Maybe I can be an actor after all.

Back to that anger stuff. I went with Mom to church

last Sunday for the first time in a while. Margie and Tobey went to Sunday school with the other kids, but I sat in for the whole shebang. The minister was on about "loving your enemy." She said something like, "Hating or being afraid of a person gives the other person power and importance, because all that fear and hating eats into us."

Like, I guess, if I'm spending a lot of time worrying about what Jeff is going to do next, I'm making him important. I hardly think he's sitting around planning what other mean things he's going to do to dorky old Alex. I should just forget about him. Shrug it off. Ignore him like Bennie does. That much makes sense to me.

Then she went on and said, "You can't be afraid of someone you love." That made me stop. If I'm afraid of Dad, does that mean I don't love him?

But I'm supposed to love my dad. We're all supposed to love our dads, aren't we? I'm sure you love yours. Right? But you couldn't love your dad if he was mean, could you? Because when I think about it, when I really really think about it, as terrible as it sounds, you know I don't think I do. Love him, that is.

In the car coming home I said, "I'm afraid of Dad. The minister said I can't love someone I'm afraid of." Mom kept her eyes on the road. "I can't even like him when he's so mean to you."

She avoided what I said about me not loving Dad. Instead she said, "I think the minister was trying to teach us how not to be afraid of someone." That sounded to me like a good start, but then she added, "If you're afraid of someone, you have to think of loving them, and then

76

you won't be afraid any more."

That didn't make any sense, in my humble opinion. And it still doesn't. But maybe that's why she doesn't get mad at Dad or why she doesn't leave him, because she tries to do what the minister says, she tries to love him. But then I'm back to the same question—how can I love my dad if I'm afraid he's going to hit me? Or hit Mom?

Oh, I don't know. It's all too confusing. Adults are confusing. I think I've said that before. Probably more than once.

Hey, I saw a red-winged blackbird today. I guess spring is coming. The sooner the better.

Alex, not Mac today

February 28

Dear Graham,

I didn't think anything worse could happen. Tobey sick, Grandma still hobbling around and now Margie. Today she climbed up into the tree fort. What a dumb thing to do in the middle of winter. And then, of course, she slipped and fell and broke her elbow. You'd think it would be soft to land in the snow, but she must have hit the root of the tree or something. She came screaming into the house. Mom took one look at her and called Emergency to say we were coming. Tobey and I went too, because someone had to look after Tobe, and I really didn't feel like being at home with Dad. Dad can't look after his own left hand.

Mom rolled Margie in a comforter from her bed and had me hold a bag of frozen peas on her elbow. Privately I thought the weather was cold enough to make its own cold pack if Margie just hung her elbow out the window. I didn't suggest it though. Tobey sang all the way to the hospital, partly drowning out Margie's crying. He was probably trying to help her. I'm not even sure he knew what was happening. But he's like that. He knew she was in pain. If the singing didn't help her, it helped me.

The nurses took her straight in, and a doctor was ready to operate when we arrived. Mom always says people complain about waiting forever in Emergency but we sure didn't have to.

It's awful seeing someone in such pain, even when it is your pain-in-the-neck little sister. It's like you want to help but you can't. It was hard, too, leaving her there.

Being Monday, I missed hockey. Yeah! By the time we got home it was about 8:20 and Dad was furious. Not only was supper not there for him, hockey was over. I didn't mind a bit. Plus, Mom had treated us to muffins and stuff at the hospital, so we weren't starving. You'd think a normal dad would have been concerned about Margie, but he only seemed worried about himself. It's going to be quiet without her running around the house like a chicken with its head cut off.

By the way, I now have a new routine when Dad is mean to me or Mom. I go upstairs and pound the bed. It's not just the bed I pound. I have a picture of Dad, a small one Mom must have taken a few years ago. I just pitch it on the bed and pound away. Dumb, eh? But at least I don't hit him. Then I would be in deep you-know-what.

I went to karate again with Bennie. Dad doesn't know but Mom does. It was even better the second time because I sort of knew what I was doing. Plus Bennie and I got to be partners.

MacAlex

March 4

Hi Gray,

I was wrong. Margie is definitely back and running around the house as fast as ever. Her cast doesn't slow her down one bit. She says she's getting all her friends at school to write on it. Tobey and me, we get to write on it only if there's room.

For March (I almost wrote February) the weather has been pretty warm and some of the frost has come out of the ground. I dug parsnips today. It's neat how they are okay in the garden all winter and taste better now than in the fall. Not that I really like parsnips. But it felt good to go out and dig. So when Mom cooked them, I ate them.

Mom came back from seeing the cancer doctor. I heard her on the phone talking with Dad in the city. It was late. Tobey and Margie were in bed. I just happened to be downstairs getting something out of the fridge.

"That's what the doctor said, Howard. You can say he's had a miracle cure if you want. I am just telling you what he said." Her voice sounded scratchy and bumpy. Then she telephoned Grandma.

When she finally got off the phone, I said, "Well, aren't you going to tell me?'

Her face was all crinkled and twisted. "Oh, darling. It's Tobey. The doctor says he has three days to three weeks to live. I can't believe it. I just can't." Her head was in her hands. I didn't know what to do. What to think. I wanted to hug her but I couldn't.

How could someone who is walking and talking die in three days like that. Sure he's tired. But I thought people died—like, you know—immediately like as if they were hit by a car. Or dragged on and wasted away until they were thin, thin, thin. How can you be sort of normal yet die of a disease a few days later. It doesn't make sense. I can't believe it either. The doctor must be wrong, has to be wrong. I sound like Dad.

...next morning
   Hi,
I didn't sleep great. I had all sorts of dreams about Tobey, flying about and drifting off. I couldn't catch him. Like he was a ghost and my hands would just about touch him then he'd dissolve out of reach. He's still asleep across the room. It's early. All I can think about is what Mom said.

me

March 6

Dear Graham

The play is going well at school. It's still rehearsals three days a week at noon. But next week we are upping it to five days a week. I'm not only going to be living-and-breathing the play, but eating-and-drinking it as well. I love it. When we're practising there's just the play and only the play. Nothing else exists.

Tobey seems to be in more pain. Mom went into Emergency yesterday. They gave her some heavy drug, morphine, she said. "Just in case." Just in case of what? He slept on the couch in the living room. Fortunately Dad is at a conference in Vancouver for a few days.

When Tobey woke up this aft, we decided to make pizza because that's what he wanted. He sat right on the counter, would you believe, while Mom rolled out the dough. Tobey still laughs from his toes right up to his belly. We all put our favourites on our own pizzas. You know me—it's onions and mushrooms and, of course, tons of cheese. I had salami too.

Tobey threw up most of his pizza.

He's sleeping now. I think Mom gave him some of the drug. He's downstairs. I am too—writing at the dining room table. It's strange, I don't want to leave Tobey. I'm even afraid to leave him. But Mom just goes about her work as normal—running in to see Grandma, making meals. How could she leave Tobey even for a minute if she thought he might die?

Poor Tobe. He must be hungry. He threw up the sandwich I made him for lunch too. At least the throw-up was on the kitchen floor, not the carpet.

Gotta run. I have to go over my lines again. There's only one place I now get mixed up. I think I'm unsure because I just run on stage and blurt out this huge long line, and it isn't related to much else that's happening. So I sort of go blank.

See ya, a

March 8

Dear G,
　　He died this morning. My little brother. Tobey.

　　a.

Saturday the 11th or 12th

something like that

G,

   Why didn't I do more for Tobey? With Tobey? He was so little. So cute. How could he die? Why didn't I believe Mom when she told me what the doctor said? Why did I want to believe Dad?

   Margie is wetting the bed. Every morning her room stinks of pee. She's really whiny. I want to tell her to shut up, but I don't. Grandma did, though. After the funeral Margie insisted that Mom pick her up and carry her. Grandma just pulled her out of Mom's arms and said, "Margaret Marie Crispin. You stop that nonsense. Be a big girl and help your mother." That wasn't fair. After all, she only just turned eight. And Tobey was her best friend. Sometimes I don't like Grandma at all. Maybe that's where Dad gets his un-niceness.

   If I'd really believed Mom when she said what the doctor said, maybe I'd have given Tobey more hugs. Would they have helped him get better? At the end, he just wanted to sleep. But I want more Tobey hugs.

   Mom walks around like she's in some far-off land. Dad looks sort of glazed over too but he went to work every day this week except Friday, the day of the funeral.

How could I ever have been glad when Tobey was asleep? How could I've wanted the peace and quiet? I miss Tobey. I miss him so much. Mom doesn't seem to notice me. I'm so glad I have these letters.

I'm not sure I'm going to be able to write much, though. I'm awfully busy with the play.

a.

March 23

Dear Graham,

It's supposed to be spring, but there's still snow on the fields and everything is grey, grey. I wish it would rain and wash all the snow away. Like me. I wish I could cry and wash all the ache away.

I'm not much in the mood to write, and I really am busy. Going over my lines takes hours and, of course, there's still hockey. Fortunately that's almost over for the season. And I'm going to karate on Thursdays with Bennie. Dad still doesn't know.

Mrs. Mayo told me I don't have to do the play if I don't want to, and she'd find someone to step in for me. But I'm glad I have the play. It's like rain. It washes my real life away. I don't think about Tobey so much. I focus like crazy on the lines and the people in the play. I can't let them down.

Last weekend I started running. I'm not sure why. To get away maybe. Or it's just that I can now, seeing I don't have to look after Tobey. It's then I think. It's then I miss him. I see his face. I hear his laugh. Sometimes I cry. I wonder why him and not me.

Every November 11th in assembly, someone reads a poem for Remembrance Day. Do you know "In Flanders

Fields"? I never thought much about the words before. But for some reason the other night I had to look the poem up in one of our books. The words made me cry. "Short days ago we lived. Felt dawn. Saw sunset glow."

I run and feel the breeze in my face and the aching pounding of my legs. Tobey can't. He can't feel the breeze on his face any more or watch sunsets or hear red-winged blackbirds.

There's another line, "If ye break faith with us who die, we shall not sleep." It goes round and round in my head. My feet jog "break...faith...break...faith." I had to ask Mom what breaking faith means.

"Breaking a promise," she said.

Did I make a promise to Tobey?

Now when I don't know what to do, I've started to ask myself, "What would Tobey do?" Doesn't that sound silly? He was just five. What would he know about dealing with Jeffrey Pinsent? Or even Dad for that matter. But somehow it helps. It makes things more clear.

Mostly I know Tobey would just laugh and be himself. He loved everything. Can I just be myself? Can I love life too? Maybe that's why I run. To feel those breezes in my face, the ground under my feet and to feel even just a little bit alive.

I don't want to forget Tobe. Ever.

I asked Dad why he never calls Mom by her proper name, Julie accented on the end with the soft j-sound at the beginning. He glared at me and said, "I can call her what I want."

What a jerk. Will I be a jerk when I grow up? Tobey wouldn't like that. I will not be a jerk.

I went to Bennie's house after school tonight for the first time. Bennie has a sister, Lydia, who plays the cello. I'd never seen a cello before. It sings with an ache in its heart. Lydia's pretty nice too. Long black silky hair that sways when she moves her head and tumbles over her shoulder when she draws the bow over her cello.

Their house is peaceful. I want to go more often. It's like I can breathe there. At my place it's like I don't breathe. For me home is a place where you hold your breath, waiting for the axe to fall. On my head or Mom's.

Sorry I'm so down. You would be too. I'm definitely glad I have you to moan to. Thanks for listening.

a.

March 25

Dear Graham,

Jeffrey Pinsent made some comment about me being a wuss, and I just plowed him one in the chin. Just one hit. Then I walked away. I think he was so surprised he did absolutely nothing. Maybe karate and running are helping me be strong. Or at least feel strong. Or maybe playing goalie. I shot my arm out just like his chin was the puck coming towards me.

That's all for now.

Mac

March 30

Dear G,

I miss Tobey. I miss Tobey. I miss Tobey. His funny words, like suppughetti for spaghetti and garbaggio for garbage. His black, black eyes. Even the browny-grey fuzz of hair he had because of the chemo. His funny way of holding his head because he couldn't see. His singing. His hand in mine.

On the Friday after Tobey died, there was a funeral. I don't think I told you about that. Actually the night before was a wake. We all had to go to the funeral home and stand in a line and smile. All the people seemed Grandma's age. I never really thought about it before. Maybe it's hard on Grandma too. Although she doesn't always show it with hugs and stuff, I guess she cares about us.

Before the wake, they had the coffin open, and Mom made us say goodbye to Tobey. That meant seeing him lying there all dressed up and perfect looking. Not like him. Not messy and wiggly. She made us touch him. He was cold. She said it was important that we really knew Tobey was dead or something like that. As if.

The funeral itself was at the church we go to, or mostly Mom goes to. It's small and in the country. The funeral place wanted us to go in a huge limousine. But

Mom as usual did all the organizing, and she got what she wanted—for a change. So we drove together in our little car, following the big car with Tobey's coffin in it. The church was completely full. Actually, so many were there that they had to put people where the choir usually sings and extra chairs at the back.

Going in was a total blur. My uncles and aunts carried Tobey's little coffin. Then we followed and sat right in the front row. I didn't like that. I wanted to be at the back, but Mom insisted we all be together. I don't remember much except the organ played a bunch of songs and the minister gave out flower bulbs. I don't know where she got the idea from, but it was like she knew Tobey. She sent big baskets of bulbs around the church, and we were all to take one. I took three. I'm going to plant mine as soon as the ground gets soft.

After the service, everyone gathered in the back of the church. Bennie and Lydia were there with their parents. A few kids came from my class with Mrs. Mayo. Even Jordan came, if you can believe it. He was with the principal and my hockey coach.

I'm worried about Margie. She's no better. In fact, I think she's worse. She sucks her thumb all the time. I can't even remember her doing that when she was really little. She carries her blankie around at home and wets her bed at night. Her elbow is still in a cast—for another two weeks I think. I don't know what she's like at school, but she's really quiet on the bus. And the big thing is that she's forgetting to feed Bronson. I do it now. Mom says to say nothing, but just to go ahead and feed him. So I do. But it still worries me. Is she getting sick too?

Mom says Margie's sad, and not to worry. But I do. I can't help it. Dad doesn't say much. He sort of stares out the window a lot. Maybe Mom's right. Maybe we're all sad in our own way.

Alex

p.s. Most days I can't even try to be Mac.

April 9

D.G.

Last night Dad came home from work as usual. Mom made a big beef stew—lots of chunks of meat and veg smothered in gravy. I like mushing it all together, the peas into the potatoes. In stew I even like turnips. Anyways, I think Mom was trying to make herself and maybe the rest of us too feel better. She set the table with a cloth and made a pie. Plus she put on a dress. Normally she's in jeans and a sweatshirt.

Dad walked in the door just as supper was ready. He took one look at her. "So who were you expecting to walk in the door, all dressed up like that?"

She had question marks in her eyes. "Why, you of course. It's Friday."

"Yeah. Yeah. I bet you get dressed up on the nights when I'm not here too, don't you?"

"I just wanted things to be nicer. For us not to be so down."

"Don't you lie to me. I bet someone was here and just left." His voice was getting louder. I felt like sneaking out of the kitchen and up the stairs, but I was stuck in the corner with Dad standing in one door and Mom in the other. Fortunately, Margie was in her room.

"What are you talking about?" Mom's voice squeaked

in a high-pitched, scared mouse way.

"I know your kind. Always sneaking around."

Mom then got into her make-Dad-happy mode. "You're tired, dear. Let's sit down and eat. I'm sure you're starved. I know I am and the kids must be. I even made you an apple pie." Dad looked down at the table. For a minute he seemed to soften. And then, like a snake, his arm shot out, the back of his hand across her face.

My face felt like the stove top on high. Like I'd been hit, not her. My ears banged inside. My chest heaved. I moved in front of Mom and said very, very slowly, "Don't you ever touch Mom again."

"Well, look who thinks he's all grown up. Big man Alex. Big wuss Alex, if you ask me. You think I'm afraid of the likes of you?" One side of his lip curled. "If you keep this up, you're next."

Then Dad sat down at the table, and Mom began bustling past me with the stew in her pot-holdered hands, putting it in the centre of the table. Margie arrived and slid into her chair with her casted arm still stuck out at a crazy angle, and I just took my place like it never happened. The dragon was definitely in the room, getting bigger, while Mom went around the kitchen with wide and watery eyes, like big buckets she was holding up, trying to prevent them from tipping over and spilling.

Sometimes I think I'm going crazy and just imagining it all. Like, it did happen, didn't it? Yet no one ever talks about it. About the dragon. It's like it's there, but it isn't. Do we continue to feed the dragon? I can't stand it any more.

This morning I got a duffle bag out of the basement and stuffed it with a pair of jeans, two T-shirts, a sweatshirt, a fleece, my wind breaker, socks, underwear and three favourite books. I also nicked some nuts, raisins and crackers from the kitchen. We go through food so quickly, Mom won't notice. Over the next while, I'll get other stuff.

This is just the beginning. I don't have a plan. But I know I'm leaving.

Mac

April 13

Dear Graham

On our way out of class, Jeff and Alan bumped into me and made some smart-ass comments about me and Bennie being the two class dorks. Carla and Brianna said together, "Quit being such jerks."

Then, wonder of wonders, Jordan hissed at them, "Oh, shove off, you guys." The rest of the class snickered. Bennie and I just ignored them.

Another piece of good news. Margie finally got her cast off. Mom said the doctor was pleased. Margie can't feel much in her fingers, and Mom is worried about that. The doctor says the feeling will come back, but it might take months. Funny, Margie looks smaller. Hopefully she'll get some of her bounce back—like go outside and roar around the way she used to. I still just give her extra hugs. But she won't let me give her butterfly kisses, probably because that was a Tobey thing.

It's quiet around here without Tobey.

I spent the weekend at Bennie's. It was great. And handy too, because we had two complete run-throughs of the play at school, one Friday night and again Saturday afternoon, so it meant I didn't have to go back and forth from the country a million times. It was the first time I'd ever stayed over at anyone's house (other than Grandma

Crispin's), and I thought I wouldn't be able to sleep. I was on a mattress on the floor in Bennie's room, but I went out cold right after the DVD. I woke when it was light and just rolled over again. The house was so peaceful.

Bennie doesn't have video games. He seemed embarrassed to admit it, but I told him my parents won't let us have them either, and I prefer reading anyways. That's when he showed me all of his books. We even played cards—all before breakfast.

When we got downstairs, Lydia and Bennie's parents had already eaten, and we just had toast and honey. Beautiful music was coming from the living room. Lydia was practising. I sneaked in to listen—and watch. Next weekend is the last before the play, and I think we're going to have a big dress rehearsal then. I hope I can stay over again. My fingers and toes are crossed so much, I can hardly walk.

a (but I am a bit Mac-ish)

April 17

Hi Graham,

The weather is sunny today. The snow's all gone. The air smells like damp earth, and the birds are loud and happy sounding. I went out tramping in Lopateckis' back fields. Most places are still pretty muddy. Beyond the hemlocks and pines are the great slabs of Canadian Shield rock, holding the heat the way they do. It was dry there and almost warm.

I did a bit of thinking. A lot actually. In all directions—Tobey, the play, Dad, the family, what's life supposed to be about. Even writing these letters.

Yes, I get a chance to say stuff. But when it goes all one way, you can't call it a friendship. That's what's nice with Bennie—it goes both ways. That doesn't mean writing hasn't been great. It has. But I'm stupid to think of you as a friend. It's make-believe. Totally make-believe. Maybe I did it because I needed a friend so badly, though I haven't told Bennie things I've told you. Like about Dad. Or my plan.

I did stay again at Bennie's. I think Lydia is so pretty. I love hearing her play the cello. Music seems to invade their house. Bennie has a guitar too and plays much better than me. Maybe one day he'll show me how to play bar chords—that's something I haven't figured out yet.

It would be neat to be able to play an instrument well. At our place, Mom used to sing a lot. I asked if she played something when she was little. She said the piano—she went as high as Grade Eight. And she sang in choirs. I asked her why she doesn't now. She didn't reply. I already knew the answer, and she knew I knew.

I planted Tobey's bulbs today. I just scratched a hole in the dirt in the front garden and put them there. I hope they grow. I need them to.

I'm getting excited about the play. Not just any old excited, but really excited. Like my mind can't focus on anything else. Think about me on Friday and Saturday! We do a run-through for the whole school on Friday afternoon, which is like the final dress rehearsal but with an audience. Then we do it again Friday night and Saturday night—for paying customers. Our gym is really small, that's why we get to do it so many times. The more times the merrier, as far as I'm concerned. I have the jitters, but Mrs. Mayo says even the greatest actors get the jitters.

Alex, the Actor

April 23, really the 24th

Hi Graham,

It's the 24th because it's after midnight. I'm curled up in bed with my duvet around me. There is no way I can sleep.

The play is over and was a huge success. Can you believe it? No screw-ups on my part and when Sarah forgot her line at one point on Friday night, my brain just slipped in with some cutesy words, and no one even noticed. Sarah afterwards gave me a big hug for saving her. That felt good.

Friday afternoon was fun because it was in front of the whole school—all the littlies, including Margie, were there to watch. How I wish Tobey could've been there. But what am I thinking? He wouldn't have seen it anyway. The kids laughed and hooted in all the right spots and afterwards came up and told us how good we were. It was neat at the end when we got flowers delivered by the kindergarten kids. Some were bubbling over with excitement to be up on stage. Others were all shy. They reminded me of Tobey.

Saturday night was the best, though. We were more relaxed and really just had a ball up there. Everything went so smoothly—from the scene changes to the musical interludes from our school orchestra (including

Lydia)—like a well-oiled bicycle, as Mom would say. After getting flowers Friday afternoon and night, us actors decided we should give some to the kids behind the scenes. We all chipped in and Sarah and Jen offered to do the buying. After Mrs. Mayo and the music teacher and the actors got their roses and bouquets, I went to the mike and called out all the backstage people.

It was such a surprise. Some were even in tears. I had to give a flower to Jeff. We actually shook hands, and he thanked me. Would you believe it? He seemed really happy. I'm not holding my breath, though, about him.

Even Dad said he enjoyed the play. Mom just hugged and hugged me until Margie wanted her share of hugs. For the first time in ages, Margie seemed her old self.

There was a party after for the whole class at Mrs. Mayo's place. First my parents said I couldn't go, but Jordan said I could get a ride home with his dad. We just sat around and laughed and talked and ate. I was starving. Mrs. Mayo had ordered in pizzas. What else? Music blared for a bit. Then Bennie brought out his guitar, and we all sang. He's good. I sat between Lydia and Sarah. It was the best night of my life, ever.

Going back to regular school is going to be difficult.

Alexander the Great Actor

Next Day

Dear G,

I knew it couldn't last long. Dad being nice, I mean. This morning Mom let me sleep in, because I got home late. She didn't know I was up even later because of writing to you. At lunch, Dad started in at me, "So I bet you think you're something after last night."

"Not really. I liked it, and other people seemed to like it too. It was fun."

"Well, don't start getting ideas."

"What do you mean ideas?" I said, pretending I didn't understand.

Mom broke in, "Oh, Howard. Leave him be. Let him enjoy the glow of success for a while."

"Ideas that you can be an actor, I mean." I figured that's what he meant. Dad's cheese sandwich spewed out between his teeth as he spoke.

"Howard. Drop it. He's only fourteen. He has a long time to think about a career."

Dad glared at both of us. He's so deflating. That's the word to use. I could feel my big happiness balloon fizzling around in smaller and smaller circles and ending in a plop of coloured plastic on the floor, wrinkled and pathetic. But I wasn't going to let him see he could do that to me. I excused myself from the table, went upstairs and did my pounding routine again. One day when I'm bigger and stronger, I will pound him out. Really pound him out. And not just his picture either.

At supper, the same thing started, almost word for word. But it got worse.

"No son of mine is going to be an actor."

"Dad, did I say I was going to be an actor? No. Did I even mention it? No. So I don't know what you're talking about."

"Don't you backtalk me," he said. "I've always known you were a wuss and a pansy. Now I know for sure."

"What do you mean by that?" I asked. Mom was pulling at my sleeve to stop. To ignore him I think.

"You know what I mean. A pansy, a homo. All actors are homos."

"Are you bigoted or just plain stupid?" I've never said anything like that to Dad before. To anyone. I guess Saturday night gave me strength I didn't know I had. Or stupidities. "And anyway, what's wrong with being gay? Nothing." I could see Dad was twitching. His face. His fists. His mouth.

I left the table without excusing myself. I shouted back over my shoulder, "Why does being gay bother you so much?" Pause. "Probably because you're afraid you are yourself." As the words left my mouth, I knew I had gone too far. Way too far.

I jammed the bolt into the lock of my door just before Dad got to me. He pounded and pounded and called me every name imaginable. I could hear Margie crying and Mom trying to calm him down. I crawled under my duvet with my earphones on. My heart ku-thudded to the music. I lay there for a long, long time. Oh, Tobey. I miss you. What would you do?

It was later, about eight o'clock, and I was lying on the bed listening to the quiet of the house when I heard Margie climb the stairs. She got just outside my door, stopped, then began whimpering. The next thing I knew Dad was bellowing again.

"What's wrong with you? A man can't relax with you blubbering like that? Are you a baby or something?" Her whimpering rose to sobbing. Then wwhhack. A high pitched scream. Silence.

I opened the door. I didn't care any more. I was already in deep trouble. In front of Dad was Margie, thumb in her mouth, one cheek flaming, her face awash in tears, jean-covered legs stiff and spread-eagled, peering down at a pool of urine.

"Don't you dare touch my sister." Arms around her middle, I dragged her into my room and slammed the door. Margie began sobbing again.

Dad hadn't even moved to grab her. "You've done it now, kiddo. You'll get it in the morning," he said through the closed door.

Mom was up the stairs by this time. I held on to Margie until the smell of pee made me want to puke. Plus she started to shiver. I had her strip down and wipe herself off with her dry T-shirt. Then she put on my pyjama tops. I cleared the clutter off Tobey's bed and tucked her in.

She's asleep now. Mom and Dad are downstairs.

All I know is I have to leave. Somehow. And it's going to have to be tonight.

Mac

April 28, Davenport

Dear Graham,

How did we get to Davenport, where I am now? It's a long story.

It was late that night. I'm not sure how late. But I waited for what seemed like forever after I heard Mom and Dad go to bed. There were raised voices for a while and finally silence. But it gave me time to think. I figured I had only one choice, mainly because I knew I couldn't leave Margie behind, not after what happened. If Mom couldn't protect her, I had to.

My plan was simple. I was going to drive the car into town, to Bennie's. Of course that's illegal and stupid— the driving bit. Under age. No license. Plus I'd never even put a key in an ignition, let alone turned one on, except in Lopateckis' tractor. But the car was my only hope. I could hardly walk to town with Margie.

First, I'd get the keys and put my duffle bag and backpack in the car. Then I'd come back for my sister.

So that's what I did. Only I didn't reckon on two things—Mom being asleep downstairs on the couch and Margie not really wanting to come and definitely not wanting to walk. Shushing Margie, I pulled a big sweater of mine over her and tried to carry her. But she was too heavy on the stairs. We slid and thumped our way down.

The next thing I knew Mom was at the bottom.

"Where in heavens are you going at this time of night?"

"I'm leaving. Here. Now." I whispered. "And Margie's coming with me."

Even in the dark, her face looked pale and frightened. I know my face pleaded, come with us, but I couldn't say it. Just as I was putting Margie's boots on, Dad peered over the top of the stairs. Mom slipped on her coat. I heard a roar, "What the hell's going on?"

I took off running, straight for the car, to the driver's side. The moon was bright, in that half-chewed in-between shape. Mom followed with Margie by the hand. But Dad must have clued in. He grabbed Mom's shoulder, and Mom let go of her. The next thing I knew, Margie was climbing in beside me on the passenger's side.

"Lock your door and the back one too," I yelled to her, as I reached behind and locked my side. I felt safer. But my heart had climbed my chest and was pumping way up in my throat. I turned the key. Would it work? Could I do it? Were we trapped? Margie was crying again and I was ready to flatten her. I had to do this. I had to succeed.

The car sputtered to life. I pulled the lever back into reverse. The little R glowed in the low light. We crept back, the car and us down the driveway. The next thing I heard was an even bigger roar out of Dad.

"You idiot. Get out of that car right now." He was by my window, pyjamas billowing, wielding a two by four in his right hand. "What d'you think you're doing? Get out right this minute, or I'll bash this over your stupid head."

Where was Mom? I willed her to come as we rolled

backwards. "Margie," I whispered. "Unlock the back door for Mom." I tried to sound calm. In my head I repeated, "Get in, Mom. Get in. Oh please. Oh please, get in." Over and over.

We moved slowly. Margie's screams rose higher the more Dad yelled and threatened. I felt a rush of cool air, a jolt on the back seat, a door slam and a click. Mom said not one word. Her hand reached forward and squeezed my right shoulder. I breathed, long and deep. In and out. In and out.

I backed up in an arc ever so slowly. As if Mom knew what I was thinking, she spoke quietly in my ear, "Go for the D" and I shifted into Drive. The car bumped and coughed, but we were still moving. This time forward. Dad jumped on the front bumper. I tried not to watch as he bounced up and down. I tried not to see his face all contorted or feel the wood wham against the hood. I tried not to wince as he flailed at the windshield. We wove our way down our lane. I almost felt sorry for him. He looked pathetic. And cold.

By the mailbox I turned left and just kept going. I'm not sure when Dad jumped off the car, but at some point he must've realized I was serious. Or maybe he was freezing and didn't want to have to walk too far. Or maybe he didn't want to be seen out and about in his pyjamas. Anyway, suddenly he was no longer bouncing along with us, and the biggest sense of relief swept over me. All I could think of was thank heavens we didn't still have Grandma's car, or he could have followed behind.

I stopped the car when we got to the next line. Without a word I opened the door, and Mom and I changed places. Mom drove straight here. To the shelter. She knew exactly where it was. Maybe she had been thinking about leaving too.

That's where we are—at the Davenport Women's Shelter. I've been going to school from here. A woman drives Margie and me and two other kids to Whistler's Corners each day. I don't like it. We have only one room between the three of us. But it won't be for long, Mom says. I've told her I'm never going back with Dad. She doesn't say a word.

a.

July 12

Dear Graham,

We're in Whistler's Corners now, in a small townhouse. I like it. I miss the space we had before—in the country, especially being outside. But I don't miss it enough to make up for the peace, the relief, the no more (as Mom called it) "walking-on-eggshells". You know, the feeling of always having to be so careful, because you never know when something's going to blow up in your face.

Anyways, we moved here just before school got out. Mom's taking a sixteen-week refresher course to become an RNA again. She was a nurse before she married Dad, but she says she's forgotten most of it. Grandma Crispin is embarrassed that her grandchildren are on welfare, so she's helping Mom with the cost of the course. Dad's supposed to pay her later, but he was never good at paying people back. Mom and Dad used to fight about it. But this time it's up to Grandma. He's her son.

Dad actually brought us Bronson the other day. It was weird seeing him again. Dad, that is, not Bronson. I kept expecting him to do something mean, but I think he's trying to pretend he's nicer now. But I know him. And I know he doesn't like Bronson's whining and mess when he forgets to feed him. Dad said he might be selling the house and moving to the city. But I think he's probably still hoping we'll move back with him. When Bronson saw us, he drenched us with slobber. I guess he missed us as much as we missed him. I wonder if he'll figure out how to open the door to this house too. I should mention it to Margie.

Speaking of Margie, I think she's a lot better, even though she's still more quiet than she used to be. This week she's at a camp for cancer kids and their families. I hope she'll be okay there. I miss her. A year ago I wouldn't have believed I'd say that, but I do. It's like I don't want her out of my sight in case she dies like Tobey.

Except for this one week, my summer job is looking after her. I wanted to work at the golf course like Bennie for real money, but Mom said she needs me here. She also says I'm too young, that I should be enjoying myself, be a kid, that I have all my life ahead of me to work. But I'm taking a lifesaving course at the pool right now so that maybe in the fall I can get a job there.

Being in town, we see lots of Grandma Crispin. I enjoy visiting her more than I used to. I'm not sure why, except now we just run in for ten minutes, and that's about long enough for all of us. Before it was always for supper. Dad would watch TV, and I had to look after the littlies while Mom helped in the kitchen. Grandma was always worried she didn't have enough food to feed us or that we'd break some of her china ornaments. Now it's sort of hi-how-are-you and goodbye and that's it.

But I don't go when Dad's there. Margie does. When she comes back, she always says she wants Dad to live with us again. She pleads with Mom, and I can see Mom weakening. I wonder if Dad puts her up to it. I wouldn't put it past him. Or maybe Grandma. Then again, it could just be that Margie's all mixed up because I'm mixed up too.

Did I cause the breakup? Would we all still be together if it weren't for me? Because I couldn't handle Dad? Because I forced us out? Deep down, I know that's not true. But I still wonder. Yesterday morning I was thinking about it. I did my usual, "What do you think, Tobe?" I asked him flat out (in my head of course). "Was it my fault?" Then that line went around in my head again—"if ye break faith with us who die, ye shall not live." Maybe now I understand what it means. I think it means that Tobey got away from his pain and blindness and cancer and those words are telling me that we have to get away from our pain too. And if we don't or if we go back, we'd be "breaking faith" with Tobey. But, oh Tobey, why couldn't you be here with us too?

Mom seems to worry all the time now, not just some of the time. And she works long hours at the hospital, which means I have to help out a lot again. So sometimes I even think it might be better if we were back with Dad again. I am mixed up. And then I remember. I remember the wildness in Dad's eyes when he gets mad, and I think of his yelling and of the nasty comments he made about Mom and about me. And I remember the eggshell stuff. We won't break faith, Tobey. No more dragon.

Guess what? Bennie and Lydia are planning a half-year birthday party for me, would you believe? When they found out I didn't even have a cake, they decided I needed a party. It's really just an excuse. It's going to be held two weekends from now at their house, and they've invited lots of people. I wonder if anybody will show up. It would be a bit embarrassing if no one came. But, hey, even if there's only Bennie and Lydia, it'll be fantastic.

I still run and when I do, I think. About Tobey and me mainly. Tobey didn't get a chance to grow and change. I get sad remembering that. Because when I think about it, I guess that's really all that living's about. Growing and changing. You never know where you'll be next year. After so many huge changes this year, I've decided I'm not going to be scared. Or at least I'm going to be less scared—less scared to try, less scared to change. I guess there's a lot more to becoming big than knowing about Santa Claus.

I miss Tobe a lot. A lot a lot. Mom says it will take years. I just hope I don't ever forget him. His laughing. Mom has put lots of pictures of Tobey around. Margie pulls them down sometimes and hides them. We find them and put them out again. I wish I hadn't planted my bulbs at the house. I won't be able to see them grow next year.

This afternoon Mom was sitting out on the back steps when I came home from running. I could feel my face dripping and my legs were glistening with sweat. We sat for a bit. Not talking. A butterfly landed on my leg. It shimmered in the afternoon sunlight, an orange glow, the colour of Tobey's hair. Mom and I stared. We didn't say a word for the longest time. It shivered and fluttered.

It was like Tobey was there, telling us he was okay. Telling us that things will be okay with us too. Does that sound crazy? I reached out. It crawled onto my palm. The strangest, lightest kiss. A butterfly kiss. And then flew away.

I shivered and trembled. Mom and I hugged.

Now I think of the butterfly and I know we'll be all right. Like Tobey.

This is my last letter, Graham. I don't need to write you any more. It's not to say writing wasn't good, that it wasn't important. It was. But I don't need to any more. I'll put this with the others in the box on the top shelf of my cupboard. One day I'll read them all again. And remember.

I'll continue to write, though. Stories or maybe songs. I might even accept Dad's offer of a two-week drama course for teens at the university next year.

Like Tobey, we'll be all right.

Alex Crispin

Acknowledgments

My writing began snuggled up with my children, imagining stories and reading books. It began as words wove enchantment in their wide serious eyes and their cheerful giggles. I am grateful to them and that magical time.

I also wish to acknowledge those many people whose lives intersected with mine to give this book substance and life.

In particular I thank the Institute of Children's Literature for encouraging my writing; Sylvia McConnell and Napoleon Publishing for their faith in *No More Dragons* and me; Tina, Linda, Lorna and Pat for reading earlier drafts; Rick for being forever a fan; and my now-adult daughter for her insightful editorial suggestions.

The book *There's No Such Thing as a Dragon* was written by Jack Kent

Rie Charles was born in the Okanagan Valley
in British Columbia. She spent much of the
intervening time in other parts of Canada and
the world. She holds a Masters Degree in social
work.

Over the years she has worked at many jobs,
including teaching and social work.

Her not-so-secret passion is writing
children's books. She always has several on
the go. *No More Dragons* is her first published
novel for young people.

CPSIA information can be obtained at www.ICGtesting.com
Printed in the USA
LVOW100334190313

324837LV00007B/21/P